D0045074

bled meeting, seeking relief from the whirling words of Morton's rhetoric.

"Words," Davis said. "They got weight with some."

"And money," Ellis said. "Hard to beat a successful man. They all feel that; most of 'em, anyway."

"Uh huh. Takes time to find what it means out here."

The pilot moved his head in a nod, and water spilled down the V again. A pause came into the talk and the two men looked down the torn embankment at the roiled mass of moving water. Midstream, three yoke of oxen had stalled, their back and shoulder muscles rigid and bulging as they breasted without motion against the tide. Behind them, the wagon swayed with the current, threatening to spill despite the dozen men who leaned upon a long line fastened to the rear of it.

"They could do with a couple, three more span of oxen on that," Davis said. "Looks like Piper's wagon."

"Likely couldn't decide as to what side of the river he was goin'," Ellis said. "Oxen comin' now, an' none too soon."

As the pilot spoke, another three yoke came through the trees on the far side and slithered down the bank, wading in now, with the water rising around them, to their hocks, sloshing along their bellies, boiling about their ribs and shoulders. The man who led them turned them slowly, standing near the head of the nigh lead ox, a massive brindle with brass knobs on the tips of his wide-curving horns.

at him; how to keep his ears from hearing the swelling tide of wagons rolling past his door; how to keep his mind from dwelling on the new green hills and valleys toward which these emigrants had set their faces. They told him not these things, nor how to keep his fists around the handles of his plow. Nor how to take with grace the refusal of a wife to journey west. Folks were always pleased to tell a man what he ought and oughtn't do, but they never told him how. He wondered if Belle was thinking of him now.

With an effort he pulled his mind away, and spoke into the sound of the rolling river and the rain.

"I keep thinkin' we should have waited. Another week, a lot of these crossin's would be down."

"I made mention of it more'n once," Ellis said.

"I heard. You'd think they'd been over the trail a dozen times."

"They'd got the fever. Won't have no checkrein on 'em."

"If that Isaac Piper they elected captain of the train had any guts, he maybe could have held 'em back."

"He had Morton pushin' on him."

"I know," Davis said, and the scene was re-created as he thought about it: Thaddeus Morton, late of Cincinnati, a man of law and consequence, haranguing the vacillating Isaac Piper, pig farmer from the Illinois River. He saw Piper wiping his nose on the sleeve of his homespun coat, looking vaguely around the assem-

"I don't look for all to be across 'til tomorrow sometime."

Ellis stood beneath the naked, barely fuzzing, branches beside the hunter. The rain water spilled in a small cascade from the V in the brim of his plainsman's hat, and softened the sweat rime of his buckskin shirt. It made the horns of his yellow mustache hang lank and wet.

"We'll take on twenty pounds in liquid weight by then," Davis said.

"Likely. Maybe we'll have sunshine for the next crossin'."

"I hope the sun is shinin' on the Platte."

"We'll get sun enough, time we're through."

The words turned in Davis's mind, and he let his thoughts go along with them—to the Platte, the South Platte, to the Sweetwater and the Green, to the Snake, to the Columbia out in Oregon. Then his thoughts returned across that distance, across the stretch of time its compassing implied, back to Independence, to the farm lying in the Missouri River lowlands; back to Belle and her vixen's smile.

Was it right that he had left her there alone? Granted she'd refused to join him going west, but was it right that he had gone without her? Folks said a man as left the trail and settled down had never ought to take the old life up again. They said this, people did, but they never told him how to keep the memories from pulling

ONE

The hunter scrambled up the sodden river bank toward the meager shelter of the trees and stopped beneath the dripping branches to await the pilot, who was coming toward him through the wagon-churned mud along the upper bank. The rain was beginning again, though it really had drizzled all day. Now it was coming heavily in gray, driving sheets which softened the appearance of the wagons wallowing across the ford below, the oxen straining in the yokes, the teamsters swinging the long bull whips, and the throng of emigrants standing by the rutted tracks, or wading in the water, heaving on the slowly turning wheels.

The sounds, too, were like the look of it, the hunter thought; muted and remote because of the hissing of the rain and the roaring of the river in flood. The shouting voices came distantly and fragmentarily, as the weird cries of far-flying birds. The rumble of the wagons coming to the ford was not discernible from the rumble of the Big Blue, and the poppers on the long bull whips, when they were heard at all, came to his ears as the sound of a small-bore gun fired from a long ways off.

"This is goin' to take awhile," Jim Ellis, the pilot, said to Aaron Davis, meat-hunter for the wagon train.

This Center Point Large Print edition
is published in the year 2001 by arrangement with
Golden West Literary Agency.

The text of this Large Print edition is unabridged.
In other aspects, this book may vary from the original
edition. Printed in Thailand. Set in 16-point Plantin type
by Bill Coskrey.

ISBN 1-58547-105-4

Library of Congress Cataloging-in-Publication Data

Prescott, John, 1919-
Journey by the river / John Prescott.
p. cm.
ISBN 1-58547-105-4 (lib. bdg. : alk. paper)
1. Large type books. I. Title.

PS3531.R434 J68 2001
813'.54--dc21

00-065964

JOURNEY BY THE RIVER

JOHN PRESCOTT

CENTER POINT PUBLISHING
THORNDIKE, MAINE

JOURNEY BY THE RIVER

Center Point
Large Print

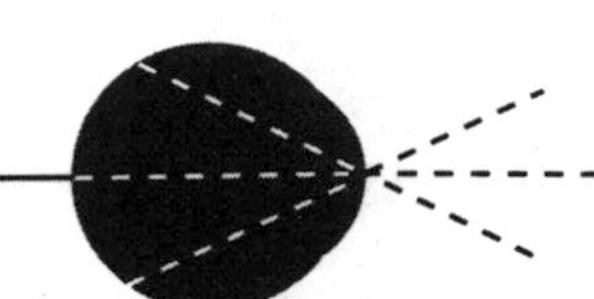

This Large Print Book carries the Seal of Approval of N.A.V.H.

ॐ श्री गणेशाय नमः

"Andy Sisson," Ellis said, and seemed to chuckle as though he was pleased with what he saw. "A good man with an ox. A lot alike, them two, but in a nice way."

More men had gathered upon the embankment now, some of them wading into the swiftly moving current, only a glance giving them the nature of the crisis. Others helped to hitch up the new spans, and still more moved along the wagon's length to heave upon the wheel spokes.

Suddenly Andy Sisson stood back and surveyed the line of animals, waved his goad at those who gripped the end rope and those who held the wheels. Then he stepped in close to his lead ox, seeming to speak to him.

From where he stood, Davis sensed the power the man held over the brindle ex. Strength welled into the creature with the words being spoken to him, and with the touch of the hand moving along his tawny neck. Davis saw no blacksnake curving out about the animals, and Sisson's goad stayed quiet in his hands.

And the oxen moved. Slow as time itself, the brindle ox pushed into his yoke, setting the others in motion as he did so. It almost seemed to Davis that the lead ox carried the others with him as his weight and power found their leverage against the river bed and applied it to the wagon. The wheels inched ahead the smallest part of a turn.

Again the wheels moved, more of the arc this time,

then paused. Then again, the oxen lunged, and retained the pressure, with the wheels going half a turn, and then a healthy full one. The wagon was moving surely now, its inclination to drift defeated. Soon the men let go the line on the rear end running gear, and the brindle ox, head low, began to rise from the water with his mate, wide streams sluicing from his body. Andy Sisson kept on talking to him as they ascended the mired bank.

"Drizzle again," Ellis said, and with his notice drawn to it, Davis realized that the heavy rain had again abated.

"Some lighter in the west," he said, looking around for the first time since the drama in the river had attracted them. "Might clear off by dark with luck."

"Still a wet camp, but there's forage, an' water at the spring." Ellis gazed through the trees, looking upward toward the prairie which lay above the valley. "You want to look around some?"

"All right. Game be gone to cover, but we're in Pawnee country, though, by forty mile." Then he stopped as he saw the mirth wrinkle Ellis's face, and he was provided with a new awareness of the pilot's easy, knowing way.

"Five years off the trail ain't so long," he went on again, self-conscious now as he slid his rifle forward so it balanced, with his hand covering the nipple where he held it; he wondered if his face showed color.

"I never said it was," Ellis said, a smile moving in

his eyes. “It was your idea.”

Davis heard his own laugh above the river’s sound. “Let’s say we both thought of it. Maybe I better take Emmet with me.”

“That’s a thought. Pawnees ain’t much, but we got a loose camp tonight.”

Davis felt the other man’s gaze still upon him as he walked off through the mud, and he retained the notion that the pilot had had himself a long look underneath his buckskin. When he entered the trees he looked around and saw Ellis leaning on his gun, his hands cupped over the muzzle of it. He was still smiling with his faded eyes.

Davis followed the river to the mouth of the creek which emptied into it near Independence Crossing. The wagons were drawn up all along the way, awaiting their turns to ford, and now that night was coming on, the men and women were making camp as best they could in the mud and drizzle. Already some of the stock had been put in hobbles and set to graze amid the woods that lined the river, and those who’d thought to carry wood between this camp and the one before were beginning to get their fires going.

Thinking about it now, he supposed his absence from this and other trails for the past five years had led him to expect some signal change in the appearance of the creek; yet when he came to the mouth and turned toward the spring he had the feeling of turning five or ten years into the past and being with Belle's old man again—with Briand Chabrun and the fur outfit in this place.

No matter the host of wagons round about him, and the scattering of blackened, ageing stumps, sign of the emigrant's axe; he could once more hear Briand's voluble Gallic laughter expressing his delight in the sycamores, elms, oaks and hackberries, which provided shade and beauty for him here. He could see the corpulent Frenchman floundering in the creek below the low falls, his hands groping in the shallows for the clams which inhabited the bottom. And he could hear the chansons of the old-time voyageurs, delicate and somehow tragic to the ear. The taste of heady aguardiente was on his tongue again.

They were calling it Alcove Springs now, and there above him, sure enough, the words were chiseled in the rock. And not far off a man named Reed, it looked like, had set his name in upon the 26th of May, 1846; a year and eleven months ago, to the day almost. So there were some changes, and this much, these names in stone, were the measure of difference between the time of Belle's old man, now gone, and this, the new day, when the once solitary place echoed to the sound of wagons rolling to the far land, rolling west.

He was caught up suddenly in something sad, something indefinite and sad, yet mighty, too, made in part of the memories now called up, and in part of the new thought.

His mind said the word again. Oregon. It rolled through his thoughts with the sound of thunder and he saw the clear image of high peaks girt with everlasting snow, of dense pine forests, and meadows deep in grass. The great Columbia flowing to the sea.

He'd never been beyond the Snake River plain, but he was going now. Goddamn it, he was going on to Oregon, on without her.

TWO

Davis and Edwards didn't encumber themselves for travel. They rode light and everything they had was carried by a pair of pack horses they'd staked out among the wagons camped at Alcove Springs. Moving toward them, Davis saw the younger man lying on a canvas tarp beneath a wagon. He was rolled in a blanket, watching languidly as Davis came through the drizzle.

"Who do we owe for the roof?" Davis stopped and looked at the wagon which gave an impression of sturdiness.

"Gideon Drew," Emmet Edwards said. "That Vermont man, an' looks it; but he's got the best damned wagon in the outfit. It's a pleasure to be under it. Have a seat."

Davis moved under, sat on a corner of the tarp and began to peel off his soggy moccasins. The name became familiar as he thought about it. Drew was on the council, he remembered now. But his place of origin remained a thing of wonder, underlining the scope of this westering migration.

"I guess even them Vermonters leave home now an' then," he said, still marveling at the thought.

"This one sure did," Emmet said. "Likely got tired plowin' granite. That's what they grow back there, I hear."

"They come from all over, I guess," Davis said.

"He was talkin' Exodus at me awhile ago; maybe that explains it."

"Must be in a travelin' frame of mind then."

Davis opened his tow sack, tossed the wet moccasins into it and pulled out a dry pair. When he slid into these he came out from underneath the wagon.

"I hope you ain't overly comfortable, Emmet," he said.

"Just tryin' to keep warm, is all. Only got enough dry wood now to cook with."

"Walkin' will keep your blood movin'. Let's go."

"In the rain? I'll be damned. I been doin' my best to keep out'n it ever since we got here."

"It ain't so bad now. We're goin' to get a sunset out of this."

"You'd never know it, the way things look. Don't

stick your neck out."

"Maybe I ain't."

Emmet came out of his blanket, rolled it and stuffed it into his tow sack. Then he picked up his rifle and powder horn, and came to his feet. "Poor weather for game. A smart buck or doe'd be folded up just like I was."

"Maybe we can find some as ain't so smart. Got everything?"

Emmet Edwards looked around, bending over to glance beneath the wagon.

"Better take the tarp," Davis said. "We can set on it if we get tired."

"Or under it if'n it pours again," Emmet said.

Davis led off, going upstream along the creek. Soon they got beyond the wagons and the animals, the sweet smoke of the wood fires and the smell of early cooking. In a while they'd be topping out, hitting the rise of prairie between the creek and the Big Blue, and the trees would lie behind them.

"We might as well go on up here," Davis said after five or ten minutes. They'd been quiet all the while, putting their energy to the climb, to the slogging through the wet, black Kansas earth, and the clinging grass.

The slope became steeper as they scaled the side of the ravine to the prairie up above. The trees thinned out and the rank bush growth fell back. Overhead, the sky seemed to press down and flow wide, spreading out toward the deepening horizons. The lush grass, nurtured by the water in the creek, shortened as the stream fell farther back, below them.

Then they came out on the rolling, grassy plain, bare and endless to the eye. The drizzle had ceased entirely now, and in the west the sky showed misty blue through large rents torn in the ragged, scudding clouds.

"This is all right," Davis said. "Let's set awhile."

"We let the game come to us?" Emmet asked the question, then shrugged, without inquiring the reason. He threw the tarp on the ground, and they sat on it. Davis felt the earth soft and spongy underneath, and saw the grass greening with the spring rains, shining brilliant through the varnished brown of last year's growth. Overhead, a wedge of geese honked north.

"Damn me," Emmet said suddenly. "It *is* comin' to us."

Davis turned around and looked east. He saw the Pawnees top out on a rise far off, ride across the swell of land, and get out of sight again in a shallow dip.

"Looks like it is, don't it?"

A quirk turned up a corner of Emmet's mouth, but he kept looking east. "You know about this?"

"I had an idea, is all; it's a good time of day for it. They're likely hungry. I guess Ellis had the notion, too." He saw the pilot's eyes wrinkle up again, the mirth and speculation as he set the bait for him.

"We learn things all day long, it looks like," Emmet said.

"Don't it, though?" Davis said, and now, as he watched the Pawnees appear and disappear with the contour of the land, he was conscious of a sense of great relief, of feeling gratified at seeing them, as though an old-time skill, long untested, had been put to use again and found still ready to demands that might be made upon it.

He was glad to see them coming when and where he'd sensed they would, and for a moment it was like the old days, the five years of marriage still to come. It was like a tonic seeing them, and his mind said, hell, thirty-five wasn't bad; Ellis would be pushing fifty. Thirty-five wasn't bad, and whatever came was a sight better than plowin' up the steamy Old Muddy bottom-lands. Now that he was getting back to it, it was; even though he was rusty yet, after five long years of staring at a mule's backsides behind a plow.

There were five horses showing themselves again, wretched in appearance even at that distance, three of them lugging travois heaped with squaws, children and folded lodges—with braves upon their backs. The other two were ridden by bucks, as well, and loaded, too, with odds and ends. They stood out some yards before the other three, leading. A pack of Indian dogs, whose yelping now was clear, ran here and there in wild disorder.

They were coming into good view and Emmet lay

on his belly, parting the stalks of grass to look at them. Davis turned to watch his study of them, and as he thought about the youth of Emmet he was glad he hadn't said what they were coming up here for. He was hardly more than a kid, with sandy hair and freckles, and a wide and friendly face; an open manner, with an eye of easy humor on the world.

But there were other things to be discovered. When he'd joined as second hunter his own say-so'd had him over the Santa Fe Trail, though never along the Overland toward Oregon; and maybe it was a good time to sound him out.

When Emmet became aware that Davis wasn't going to speak, he looked at him and smiled in recognition of what he saw. "I call it, huh?"

"Might as well, if you feel like it. Little practice won't hurt none."

"Why not? You was likely wonderin' about me, anyway."

Emmet took a breath, and let it out of him as he spoke into the quiet stirring of the prairie grass.

"I figure they just come out of their winter village, an' is headed off somewheres on a hunt. Don't seem to me they'd be lookin' much for trouble, what with squaws an' kids bein' along. I got a notion they seen the train headin' for the crossin', an' is comin' in to beg, an' maybe steal a little."

Emmet stopped talking, but kept his eyes on the

Indians. In the time that he had taken, they had come closer, and the squalor of their condition was obvious. They were going on a long slant down the ridge of prairie that lay between the river and the creek, and their line of travel would bring them to the crossing, where they could camp, if they wanted to.

"We called it about the same," Davis said.

"I ain't much on Pawnees," Emmet said. "On the Santa Fe Trail it was mostly Arapaho, Apache, Cheyenne, Comanche an' Kiowa. Osage, too. Others sometimes showed up to trade at Bent's Fort on the Arkansas. But it don't look to make much difference in this case."

"No, I don't guess it would," Davis said, and he was aware that Emmet was trying to make a showing for himself. He waited a minute before he spoke again. The Indians were almost opposite by a hundred yards and he saw the scrawny look of the ponies, the tattered buffalo robes the men were wearing, and the heads shaved up to the ridges of hair that ran from front to back.

"Sorry-lookin' lot," he said after the pause. "The pox cut 'em down one time, an' they're always goin' at it with the Sioux. But they'll steal you blind if they get the chance."

"An' do worse if they get you on the trail alone, I hear," Emmet said. "Do you reckon they'll try anything with the wagons scattered to hell an' gone, the way they are?"

"I doubt it. Maybe get their hands in the cookin', or anything lyin' loose. It'll be all right if folks keep their heads. Ellis can handle 'em."

"More'n a few'll have their own ideas, I'm bettin'."

"Uh huh. I expect we'll hear from Morton."

"He's a pretty big man, ain't he, Aaron?"

"In Ohio he was, they say; but he's a long way out now."

"One in every outfit," Emmet said. "The less they know, the more they try and run things. He's got a nice lookin' wife, though. Must be dull livin' with a man havin' twenty years or so on her. I wouldn't mind spendin' some time in the wagon with her."

"That's an interesting thought," Davis said, and he let it go at that. He had the notion that Emmet would enjoy an intimate discussion of Molly Morton, who was surely qualified for it, but when he thought of her he got ideas; and that was a bad thing, with Belle sitting in his mind the way she was.

The Indians had passed now, and Davis changed the subject. "Maybe you better get on down an' tell Ellis what's comin'. I think I'll tail 'em in."

They were backing off the tarp, keeping hunched, taking no chance of being seen.

"All right," Emmet said. "I'll have the coffee going, too."

The younger man slid off toward the ravine behind them, and Davis waited until he disappeared. Then he stood up and walked out through the prairie grass. It was wet and clinging, still, but the sun was breaking through, and the wide plain, bathed in rain, looked as clean and unmarked as the day that God had laid it out.

It gave him a lift, as the Pawnees had, and he felt a smile coming on his face. He had the sudden, odd notion that he was walking in a new land, a new world, where no one else had ever walked. Just then he was feeling the best he had since they had started out.

When he saw them again the Indians were entering the fringe of timber reaching upward from the river, still a mile or more from where the wagons camped. The sight of them gave growth to old thoughts, and he remembered other times and places when the Pawnees had come to call.

He remembered times when they'd descended on the old camps in a swarming gaggle of chattering squaws and kids, ravenous dogs and stringy ponies with forelocks in their eyes. The bucks would squat around the white men's fires, their robes about them, legs encased in black and greasy buckskin, begging tobac, begging food, eating anything and everything with relish. And all the while the squaws and kids aprowling, prying into tents and tow sacks, picking up anything they found loose. Some of them squaws could get an ox beneath their skirts.

It gave him pleasure to hark those memories up

again, and a pleasure, too, to follow the trail of these Indians ahead. To track air Indian, unseen and unsuspected, through the country was asking something of a man. He was calling again upon the sly craft, and it made no difference that these were only Pawnees come to beg a meal, and not a bunch of Sioux with their faces painted black.

When the trees moved around him he saw the Indians going on a long incline through the timber, heading toward the crossing. He was in a high, clear place just then, before the woods darkened down below, like a bluff almost, higher some than the land around it, heaped up on an easy bend in the river, with a fair view both upstream and down.

The sun was coming across the tops of the trees, and cast long planes and shafts of light through the trunks and branches farther down. Deep in, close to disappearing once again, the Pawnees moved onward in their line, shadow-mottled, the travois jerking through the brush, and the squaws and children not riding any more, but scurrying along on foot. They had it set in mind to arrive in time for dinner.

Slowed to look below, Davis saw the sinking sun turn the angry, silt-shot river honey-brown, with curls of silver where it caught in spinning whirlpools or broke in crests on brush or fallen trees; pausing here and there to catch its breath, then plunging on again. Through the small buds and early leaves, he could see activity far up at the crossing.

They looked to be moving stock across the ford. The animals were far off, bunched in dark blots, hesitating so that he could sense their apprehension; the broken line of them sagging down in deeper water, then rising up again as bottom rose beneath them on the other side.

As he watched he saw a knot develop in the center of the ford. It looked to be some balky critter'd froze and brought them piling into one another. He saw the bulge develop and the riders coming in to clear it, and then it seemed to come apart of its own accord, the most of it resuming the slow and careful movement on across. Hard to beat stock for bein' womanish sometimes.

Then he saw that something had come apart. Like a bead on a broken string, a critter slipped out of line. It moved slow when the ford was still beneath its feet, but rapidly once the current had its way with it. In the manner of great hands, the tide immersed it, turned it round and round and cast it up again, repeatedly, sweeping it along upon the turgid flood.

Without thinking of it, Davis went to the edge of the bluff where the view was broad and unrestricted. For a moment the bulk of the promontory at the bend obscured the moving blot, but when it reappeared across the river he could then make out the narrow skull, and the ears longer than a horse would have.

It was a poor damned mule, all right, but now come

back from first panic, it was striking out for the distant bank. The current had carried it away beyond the sight of those upriver at the ford, but it looked to have a grip on things, and a foot at a time its thrashing brought it nearer to the overhanging trees. To watch the struggle put Davis in mind of the river's power, and he wondered what it must be like to grapple with it; what dumb terrors must assail a mule when thus entrapped and rushed along.

Then he saw the animal strike bottom strike, slide off and strike again, and this time stay. He gave a snort, satisfied that it was on solid earth, and turned away, but stopped again as a shadow of motion caught his eye. He looked full at the spot on the wooded shore beneath him and saw the Pawnee buck ride through the tangle of brush, and poise his horse upon the bank. When the mule lurched into the trees on the other side, the buck began to swim his horse across.

The sun was down now, and the shadows moving through the camp drew little definition from the quickly failing light. It was just that time of day when things were hard to see, before the campfires were much help. Going past the wagons toward the crossing, Davis smelled the dinners simmering in the Dutch ovens, and in the iron stoves that some had brought along; savory dishes put together by a woman's hand. Woman's talk, chatty over cooking, drew his ear these days. Likely a part of him was harking back to Belle.

"I swear, I don't have a cracked egg yet; they do ride well in cornmeal."

"I'd like to bury my head in it 'til we finish these infernal crossin's. It's like to bust, itself."

"It won't be long before we're rid of them. That Mr. Ellis says were goin' to be in buffalo country one of these days."

"My Henry's surely lookin' forward to it; always had a taste for wild meat, Henry did."

"Jamie! Don't you go down by them savages! They'll likely cook you up like one of them dogs!"

"Nice water at the spring, here. On a ways it's s'posed to have critters swimmin' in it."

"Bile it, Maybelle. Coffee an' tea is what to drink."

"I never saw such rivers in my life. They don't behave this way in Vermont. They keep their place, like any proper person."

Somewhere a nest of kettles spilled and fell. Davis heard them clashing on the earth, and saw one faintly rolling on the slope, a dark shape, gathering momentum. Like a grounded cannonball, it surged and bounded wildly, and Davis paused. Then it swerved and was on him like a questing hound. He was leaping and falling all at once, with his foot ensnared by the handle and the mud pressed cold and wet against his body. A woman's voice was calling out at him.

"Where are you going with my kettle?"

Davis pushed with his hands and felt the mud squeeze out between his fingers. He came to his right foot, and leaned against a sycamore to remove the kettle from the other. It was dark and slippery underfoot, and the woman was still calling out to him.

"Where are you taking my kettle?" the woman asked of him again.

"Nowhere," Davis said. "It was the other way around."

"I see you down there," the woman said, persisting.

First she was a voice, becoming gradually a form at the tailgate of a wagon, looking out. Davis saw her faintly against a campfire's glow as he slogged upward with the kettle banging at his leg. When he was close enough he realized that Molly Morton's kettle had tripped him up.

"Oh," she said, and it was not belligerent any more. "Why, Mr. Davis—it's you!"

"Yes, I guess it is, at that," Davis said. He came up the slope and saw her clearly in the firelight and shadow, looking outward from the wagon. "Who did you think it was?"

"Oh, dear; I don't know. An Indian, I suppose. Thaddeus says they steal everything they can."

"Do I look like one?" He held the kettle in his hand, not knowing exactly what to think. He was very much aware of her somehow.

"Not now, but you were in the dark before," she said,

and when she did not immediately go on Davis remembered the mud again, and saw the amusement beginning in her eyes. "But you look pretty awful just the same," she added after the pause.

"Takes a pig to look good in mud," Davis said, and began to scrape off the muck, wiping his hands and face on a rag she handed him. "An' that only to another pig."

"Why, I do believe that's so," she said, and when he looked again he saw her small teeth white against her lips with the laugh beginning, and her eyes becoming alive with it. "I'm sorry. I don't mean to be rude, but I thought plainsmen were so sure-footed."

"It ain't usual they have to find their way through kitchenware," Davis said. He was enjoying this. "Maybe I ought to roll a kettle down on you."

"Would you feel better then?" Molly Morton said.

"I'd have to wait and see," Davis said, and he was laughing himself now. She was estimating him, and teasing him a little, too, and he liked the spirit of her. He remembered Emmet's observations, and appreciated them.

Someone called from off a ways and when she turned her head the line of her throat and lifting breast lay clean against the light, and he was aware of her again.

"It's Nellie Piper. She's always wanting something. I'd better go."

"All right. Here—wait." Davis stooped again, and gathered the other pots and kettles and passed them up.

"Thank you," Molly Morton said, and her smile this time did not seem to have remembrance of his rolling in the mud.

"Good-bye."

"Good-bye," Davis said, and he walked a ways before she brought him up again. He saw her clear against the fire as she called, and heard the humor in her voice.

"Watch your step," she said; her laugh was musical.

"Obliged for the thought," Davis said. "An' watch your kettles."

Near the crossing Davis passed the Indian camp. They had their lodges pitched, smoke curling up through the openings where the poles crossed, the hide coverings giving out a soft glow from the fires built inside. The women and children were sidling here and there, getting into things. The bucks were standing around wrapped up in their robes, talking in their chests to one another the way they did; a sweep of the arm at the swollen river; a nod at the prairie schooners gathered on either side; a finger pointing at the mules and horses, and the whoa-haws with their curving horns; a chorus of shaking heads at the whole idea.

Davis idly noted the absence of a Pawnee horse. And sure enough, a squaw was cooking up a young pup, too.

Emmet Edwards had brought a tow sack from the Springs, and he and Ellis had a fire going in a clearing close to both the crossing and the Indians. Davis smelled the bacon cooking in the Dutch oven as he squatted down beside them. It looked as if Emmet was getting ready to put his biscuits in.

"Coffee?" Ellis said. "Give the man a can, Emmet."

"Thanks," Davis said. He took the hot can in his hand and looked around. "Through for the night?"

"Looks like. A mule went down the river a while back an' broke things up. A crowd went after it. It belonged to Sisson."

"I seen it," Davis said. "He climbed the other bank, 'round the bend." Then he told the two men about the Pawnee cutting after it.

"Be a big surprise when they all meet up there," Emmet said.

Ellis looked out from under the brim of his hat at the Indian lodges. "Head man over there is old Antelope. I knowed him before. He's all right. Them with him is mostly relatives. They're goin' to buffalo."

"A strayed-off mule won't change that?" Davis said.

"I doubt it. They don't want no trouble. Likely we'll get it back if the buck got to it."

They ate the food that Emmet fixed, and sat around the fire with their pipes, simply lazing. The Indians were circulating, begging food, trying to swap for portions of the boiled dog. Ellis gave an old crone the bacon rind in trade, but buried the dog part when she turned away.

"It ain't that I don't like it; I've et it plenty. I'm just full up, is all." Ellis was smiling and Davis wondered what he was thinking of—if his mind was here or off along some other trail miles away and years ago. He was like that, Davis thought; it was hard to tell.

Davis felt his full belly bring drowsiness upon him. He let his eyes meander here and there, seeing the fires close around them, and others winking through the trees from farther back. A kind of pause was settling on the camp; dinner was being finished, dishes cleaned, the children put to bed. For the first time in the day the women were relaxing, moving about the wagons, visiting with one another.

A number wandered down to look at the Indians, gathering in the clearing, wanting perhaps to go nearer to the tipis, but wondering, too, if that was the thing to do. Like hens they peered and stretched and clucked among themselves, speculating on the nature of those squalid people. They were not Sioux, by any means, the women had been told; but neither were they Kaws. Still, they did not appear dangerous, sitting around the way they were.

Davis watched the women casually, feeling relaxed and easy by the fire. His eyes fell on the Morton woman, come to mingle with the others, and he thought of Belle, her soft arms about his neck, her body close.

Or was it Belle? She and Molly Morton were in his mind together now; they were different from each other, yet there was a likeness, too, more of manner than appearance. The unconscious provocation of Molly Morton suggesting Belle's dark flame of passion; the restless eye, the shadowed underlip, the handy figure. What difference if her hair was strawberry, copper-haloed in the firelight?

He let his eyes drift off, but they returned again, and met with hers across the campfires in the clearing. He could not say exactly what this sizing-up might hold for him, but there was a smile, for sure, and perhaps an invitation.

THREE

I be dogged, they got the mule," Emmet Edwards said. "Or it's got them; kind of hard to tell."

Davis came to his feet at sight of the commotion on the other side. He saw the mounted riders and the mule all turning and cavorting. Sisson, the emigrant from Indiana, had the mule on a hackamore, but Thaddeus Morton and Isaac Piper, the train's captain, were trying to drive it into the water from behind. There was another pair of men that Davis didn't know, and altogether the moving shadows and forms appeared grotesque in the strange contrast of firelight and darkness.

"What the hell," Emmet said. "They ought to stake it over there."

Everyone was standing now, and others were coming to the clearing to watch the show. Sisson had got the animal in the river and the campfires made its eyes blaze red with fear and rage at the feel of the water surging up. Its back heaved and the hooves went lashing sideways. Morton kept thumping on its rear end with his rifle stock, but it was going to take its own sweet time in crossing over, and mortal power would have little or nothing to do with it.

Once it got the feel of land beneath its feet again, it calmed as if nothing had happened. Sisson got down and hobbled the legs, and the mule stood blowing and looking wall-eyed while it got used to the earth again. Now that it was over, the Hoosier Sisson seemed to regard the matter as a joke, but some of the others had the air of men who had accomplished something. There was a look of bellicose triumph in Morton's eye that made Davis wonder about the Pawnee who'd crossed the river. He had his rifle resting in the curve of his elbow as though he'd done some business with it.

The voices were coming now, and someone said, "Y'ought to leave that bloody-eyed beast a mile out in the prairie."

When Sisson got to his feet he seemed embarrassed to find himself the center of attention.

"I was for it," he said, "but Piper's our wagon captain and he said to bring him over where the Indians was camped."

"To confront them with the evidence," Thaddeus Morton said, and he made himself important with the sound of it. "One of these savages was running this mule off when we apprehended him."

"Aw, now, Morton." The Indiana man was smiling and being apologetic, as though the whole thing had got to be some kind of misunderstanding.

"Well, you saw it, Sisson. He was going after your mule, chasing him toward the east."

Sisson laughed, affable and easy with the notion.

"Hell, he wasn't no closer to it than we was. I doubt he was runnin' it off."

"Sometimes they head east from pure cussedness," someone said, and Davis recognized the deliberate, nasal voice of Gideon Drew.

"Them that's bought along the Muddy sometimes do," another man said. "Given they ain't too far along the trail."

"I got him in Independence, as a spare," Sisson said. "And I cussed the day more'n once since then."

Morton waved this all aside, and took up where he'd left off. He looked as if he were addressing a jury, back in Cincinnati, and aimed to make a thing of it. "Did he stop when I fired at him?" he asked, and then he turned on Isaac Piper, who stared slack-jawed at the fire. "How about it, Piper?"

Piper looked up vaguely, and Morton had to repeat it for him. "I don't think so," Piper said when he had got the straight of it. "Looked to me like he kind of veered off."

"And kept on running, didn't he?" The edge of Morton's voice sawed at the other man.

Piper stared around, his hands grubbing in his pockets as though he hoped to find the answer there; then his glance fell on Sisson, and he seemed to remember something that decided him. "Ran like hell," he said, emphatically.

"Likely scared him half to death." Ellis, the pilot, spoke for the first time, and Aaron Davis saw a little smile working at his mouth. "Mostly, Indians run livestock off in the middle of the night."

"Thievery doesn't know the time of day," Morton said, as if he were well-grounded on the subject.

"I was scoutin' downriver, and seen both the mule an' the Indian," Davis said. "I figure the Pawnee knew the critter'd be looked for."

"Likely buildin' character for a good feed," Ellis said. "An' got paid for his trouble in lead."

"This may be a joke to you," Morton said, "but the rest of us in this party have property to protect. We have a right to secure it against molestation."

"I got a couple of horses in this game; I ain't exactly a pauper." Ellis' voice had a hard core underneath its softness now.

"If it comes to that, I've got three that cost well over a thousand dollars apiece," Morton said, and by the sound of it implying that Ellis and his pack animals were hardly in the running. "And I won't have them exposed. We demand to see justice done."

Sisson kicked at the ground as though that set the end to a problem he'd been wrestling with. "Speak for yourself, Morton. Me an' my mule is out of it. I ain't been convinced. Once ashore, he just took panic, an' headed for the Muddy. There was a Pawnee, sure, but he scared off without gettin' near the mule. We got the critter back, so we're all even. I see no reason to go beyond it."

"I say these Indians need a lesson," Morton said, his way with it seeming to set himself up as judge as well as jury. "We've got more than a hundred people in our care, and we owe it to them to see there's no repetition of this outrage."

"What kind of lesson?" Sisson said.

"We'll decide about that. I think the council ought to meet. How about it, Piper?"

"You're damned right." Isaac Piper under Morton's influence was getting the feel of authority now, and he was making certain Sisson knew about it. "We'll meet right now."

"The council be damned," Andy Sisson said. "You got it rigged front and back."

"Ridiculous," Morton said. "It's a duly elected body.

You ought to know that; you're on it."

"That's right," Piper said. "You got your say, like anybody else."

"For what it's worth," Sisson said. He looked around, defeat putting roundness in his shoulders. Then he said, "All right, let's meet. Let's get it over with."

The men moved away from the crowd a dozen yards or so and Davis followed them with his eyes. Whatever the question, the answer was known in advance, for Sisson would stand alone, with maybe Gideon Drew to side him, but that was all. It was a matter of personalities now, the issue being secondary, and Piper and Morton would vote together, with the power of Morton's wealth and character likely to carry Edgar Mabry over, too. Maybe Mabry'd had his own mind one day, but he had a numerous family, too, and his eye ahead on Oregon. Morton would be an influential friend to have in that new and distant land.

Jim Ellis, the guide, looked into the fire and sucked on his pipe, and Davis wondered where his mind was wandering now.

"What do you think?" he said to him.

"Hard to tell. Piper and Morton're pretty well ganted up."

"Can't you get in on it and talk sense to 'em?"

The pilot shook his head. "I'm only a guide, Aaron; a hired hand. I ain't been duly elected to the body."

Ellis tapped his pipe on the heel of his hand, and

stood up. “I ain’t called on Antelope yet,” he added. “I’ll be back.”

Ellis moved away, and the hunter let his eyes go after him, and on ahead to the Indians hunching by their fires. They were quiet and settled down, not mixing any more, as though they had the scent of something and were staying close together until they understood it. When he looked over at the council meeting he saw Andy Sisson pick a big gob of mud from off the ground, and slam it down again. Then he rose up and came back across the clearing.

“Where’s Ellis?” he asked Davis, coming up to him.

“He went to call on Antelope. What’s doin’?”

“They aim to give the head man the lash.” Sisson stood with his hands on his hips, blowing like his mule had done.

“That’s Antelope. What in hell for?”

“An example. The buck they want got scared off and ain’t come back, but they got to have a goddamned example. Me an’ Drew was outvoted. They had Mabry with ’em.”

“That’s a pretty big order,” Davis said. “Who thought it up?”

“Morton, I guess. He put Piper up to it.”

Davis turned it over in his mind, marveling at the ways of men of little knowledge, little understanding, depending on a guidebook for what they knew of the way to Oregon. He remembered now that Piper had got himself the captaincy that way, spouting off his learning to those who'd got to Independence after him. Likely Morton could have had the job, no matter that Piper'd had the time to make himself known to others, but like as not it appealed to Morton's vanity to find that he could maneuver Piper to his way of thinking.

He looked away from the fire and Sisson, who stared his anger into it, to the Pawnee lodges, to the crowd biding its time with quiet talk. He saw the old Pawnee, Antelope, standing alone, wrapped up in his shoddy robe, his leggings torn and stringy. He found Ellis drifting through the gathering, followed him over toward Sisson's mule, where he lost him again, until he returned to the fire. Then the meeting broke up, and the other council members came walking back.

"They figure to whip old Antelope," Andy Sisson said to Ellis.

"I heard," Ellis said. "Bad medicine."

"And why?" Morton, Piper and the others had come up, and Morton confronted the pilot with the question.

"One thing, Antelope ain't done nothin'. For another, you can't whip a chief an' get away with it."

Morton gave a hard, impatient laugh. "My God, man, we outnumber them fifteen to one."

"You'll have the whole Pawnee nation on us 'fore we reach the Platte."

Davis had his eye on Ellis, and now he saw the guide step back, as though to give the people a better view.

Then he reached beneath his buckskin shirt, withdrew what he'd concealed there, and held it up. The streaming hanks of hair glistened black and shiny in the firelight. Ellis raised it high, and pitched his voice to be heard by everyone.

"This here's a Sioux scalp, took by Antelope hisself! Figure how your own, or maybe your kid's'd look strung on a Pawnee lance!"

Davis took a look around and saw the shock go through the wagon people. He wondered what he saw the most of, revulsion or fascination, in the faces straining inward to see what Ellis held. Then he heard the growing murmur, and saw Piper shuffle in the mud, his ears attuned to it. Mabry's face was screwed up like a frightened rabbit's. Morton jammed his hands in his trouser pockets, and scowled, but he listened, too. Old Antelope stared impassively from his tipi, and Davis had the queer thought that a breath of humor touched his face.

"You can't do it!" someone shouted.

"No, by God, you can't!"

"Too danged dangerous, and it ain't right, nohow."

Ellis put the trophy beneath his shirt again, and the murmurs and the early, isolated protests became a clamor as the crowd closed in to argue with the council. Without its even being put to an actual vote, the whole idea of flogging old Antelope was dropped. Ellis came back to the men gathered at the fire.

"I be dogged, that learned 'em," Andy Sisson said.

"You got the crowd behind you, anyway," Emmet Edwards, the assistant hunter, said.

"It bothers me that my mule should be the cause of it. I should have bought another ox instead." Sisson was smiling, sustained in what he thought was right.

Ellis watched, amused-like, and put his hand beneath his shirt again. Mostly, the wagon people were away from them a few yards, their backs turned.

"Your mule's worth somethin', Andy. He gave me this."

He held aloft the streaming hanks of black hair which he had represented as a Sioux scalp. Sisson took the strands, staring at them.

"Antelope ain't counted coup on a Sioux in ten years; I had to take my own scalp offen your mule."

"I be dogged," Sisson said, and then he laughed in loud guffaws.

"Not so loud," said the pilot. "Don't ever let 'em get onto this."

Ellis took a long look through the crowd before he spoke again, and Davis had the notion he was taking the measure of Morton and Isaac Piper as they tried to mollify the anger of the other emigrants.

"Be dogged, if you want," he said. "Be careful, too."

"Careful?" Sisson looked at him.

"I'd keep an eye on Piper, if I was you."

FOUR

The Big Blue of Missouri, the Wakarusa, the Kaw, the Red Vermillion, the Black Vermillion, the Kansas Big Blue, the Little Blue, and all the named and nameless creeks that struggled into them. In nearly a month of travel you became confused in trying to keep them straight, Molly Morton thought, especially those Blues, of which there seemed to be so many. But each would be remembered in the ache or bruise, the lavender or greenish mark upon her hips or ribs, acquired in the fording of it; and the journey was hardly beginning, so the pilot said. Still, they would reach the Platte today, and that seemed to be something of an occasion.

She straightened on the rocking seat to look ahead. The shining canvas tops of the covered wagons dipped and soared majestically in the brilliant sunlight. It was so nice to have it warm and sunny for a change, the thought occurred to her. One became so weary of rain falling endlessly from lowering skies, of clothing feeling always damp, and one's own hands and feet forever cold and clammy. And it was depressing to the spirit, too.

Today, a soft breeze carried the scents and smells of the open prairie on it, the vague dry smells of last year's withered grasses, a now-and-then putrescence from the buffalo wallows they passed from time to time, and the soft and optimistic smells of spring growth reaching for the sun, the wildflowers coming into bloom. The Lord only knew where the wind began, it was so big and wide out here. Everything had changed since they had left the knolled and wooded valley of the Little Blue in back of them, and the mind had to search to put a proper measure to it. The forested and closed-in East had nothing to compare with it that she could think of.

The breeze lay on her face, and stirred the waves of strawberry hair that fell along her neck. She relaxed again, luxuriating, content and almost drowsy, like a cat before a fire; wondering, as she allowed her mind to drift, how the feel of it might be upon the whole of her, devoid of clothes, exposed to the warm caress of it.

A wanton thought, and her mind took pause to ponder the novelty of it. She could not remember being inclined toward any such thing before, much less dwelling to pleasurable extent upon it. Certainly not in Cincinnati. Had the wild, extravagant vastness of this country touched some notionous chord in her? Or was it something else?

Far ahead, she saw her husband riding horseback with a group of other men, sitting stiff and square, aloof somehow, his vanity still smarting from the business at the Big Blue crossing two weeks back. Poor Thaddeus. Something had gotten into him, all right. She had grown accustomed to his officious ways, his belief in his own infallibility, but this was different, alien; cropped up since they had left the settlements behind. And if not alien to his nature, latent, perhaps—which was worse by far—lying dark and secret for who could say how long.

Would he have flogged a tattered old man before, Indian or not? And now that he had learned of it, why could he not take the mule tail in the spirit which most of the others had?

The question formed in her mind, and the implication reflected upon herself. Quite suddenly, she understood she did not know Thaddeus very well; in fact, no better now than on her wedding day more than a year ago. Had she ever loved him? No. She doubted it, was sure of it; but she'd respected him, and who in Cincinnati hadn't? And such flattery to have the distinguished man pay court to her. Her father's best cigars and finest cordials had testified to that; Miss Herring's Female Seminary all of a dither for weeks on end.

One married, after all, whether love was there or not, when the match looked promising and one was nearing twenty.

An alien sound, at variance with the creaking of the axles, the clanking of the trace chains and the plodding of the oxen, distracted her, and she leaned outward, looking back. Aaron Davis was coming forward past the wagons at a canter—and she, good heavens, without her bonnet on, her hair atwist in the breeze.

"Good morning!" His voice carried out above the drumming of the hoofs, and the sorrel horse caracoled in a flare of flying mane and tail as Aaron Davis turned and reined it in beside the wagon. He swept his hat from his head, and Molly saw his white teeth and his tanned face and the frame of curly, dark hair, and thought, "Oh, dear," and nearly said it out loud, too.

"Hold on there, Bess," the handsome hunter was saying to the little mare. "Easy, gal."

"My, she's frisky," Molly said. Caught by surprise, she thought the pretty mare a safe and neutral subject for the moment. "Is she always that lively?"

"Sometimes she is, sometimes she isn't. She's a woman; maybe that explains it." Aaron Davis laughed. "I think she likes the weather today. That and the way the country's opened up."

"It *is* big, isn't it? I don't think I ever saw so much land all at once before. Or sky."

"Wait 'til you see the Platte. It'll make your eyes ache."

"How far now?" she asked; and as Aaron Davis stood in his stirrups to look ahead, her fingers fluttered through her wind-swept hair, and smoothed her gingham skirt. What a sight she was!

"Right up there," Aaron Davis said. The fringe on his buckskin shirt jiggled as he held his arm out, pointing.

Molly stared into the hard, bright light, and saw the

range of hills rising on the horizon, distantly.

"It looks far. Will we get there by night?"

"Afore that. We'll likely noon there. Them hills are dunes, mostly; some grass an' sage on 'em, an' cactus. Ain't so high as they look."

"Oh," Molly said, "they look awful high to me."

"It's just the country bein' so flat," Aaron Davis said. "An the air so clear."

"It even seems to breathe better," Molly said, and quickly thought, "Oh, dear, how silly I must sound." But he had spoken to her only twice before, and never as long as this, and she didn't want him to go just yet. Then a new thought came to her, and she said, "Are there buffalo nearby? I've been looking at their wallows."

"Mostly further west, but likely there's a few around. Me an' Emmet're goin' out in a day or two to have a look. Y'ever eat buffalo?"

His grin told her he knew the answer, and was likely making fun of her; but wasn't that encouraging?

"No," she said, "but I'd like to try some, though. Is it good?"

"Most like it, once they get the taste. The cows are the best."

He shifted around in the saddle, as though he might be seeking out a buffalo right then and there, and she took the moment his eyes were away to right her skirt again; wondering now if he thought her acting high and mighty wearing gingham instead of linsey-woolsey as most of the other women did.

"I hope it's cow, then, if Thaddeus and I get any to eat."

"If me an' Emmet have luck, you likely will. It's our job to keep the train in meat." He looked away again, and smiled, as though a joke had just occurred to him. "But even the bulls are good for somethin'. We put 'em all to work."

"You do?" she said, and then quite suddenly recalled what the pilot had told Thaddeus about the lack of fire-wood upon the plains, and what one used in place of it. She felt blood rushing through her face, and she said, "Oh!" abashed.

But if Aaron Davis noticed, she couldn't tell, for he was gone again before she could judge his face. Gone as he had come, his hat in a wave, and the mare's tail flying. She stared after him, oddly empty, yet with a sense of fullness, too; pleased that he had stopped to pass the time of day, yet wondering why he had.

Was something he had seen in her responsible for his gaiety? Or was it the look of the day, the country spreading wide at last, and the Platte just over the rise of hills? She'd watched him many times before, in secret. Sometimes he seemed gay and carefree, other times preoccupied, and even melancholy, as though he had a problem in his mind to trouble him.

She turned their conversation over in her mind,

seeking clues, finding nothing. But merely thinking of it was a breathy excitement, strange to her, and a spice of laughter when the end of it returned to mind.

Poor Thaddeus, she thought, but failed to feel the compassion connoted by the word. With clarity, her mind could see him stalking toward the wagon, his nose atilt in pride. His arms filled with the dry, flat chips of buffalo dung.

Folks sure was acting childish today, Isaac Piper thought. You'd think they was goin' to get to Oregon itself, an' it was just the Platte. If they'd all read the guidebook, like himself, they'd know it wasn't nothin' to take on about. A poorly length of land, he'd read it was, fit for little anyone could put a name to; with cholera an' camp fever lurkin' by to strike you down. With Indians everywhere, Sioux they was, too. An' then them awful Mormons maybe goin' along the trail aside you. On the north bank, granted, but that was close enough.

Ellis, in his soft and quiet-smiling way, said it wasn't half that bad, but if he knew so much, why didn't he write a guidebook, too?

Now there was a bunch gathered around the pilot, all looking solemn an' polite, while he answered questions for 'em. Piper heard Gideon Drew's voice asking, "Half an hour, about?"

"Close to it," Ellis said. " 'Less the dunes has moved

around since I was here last."

The pilot smiled, like the thought of such a thing might be a joke, but Sisson took him up on it, looking oxlike as he spoke, Piper thought. "Moved?"

"Sometimes they change shape, the bare ones, from the wind blowin' on 'em."

"You figure we'll noon at the hills, Jim?" Emmet Edwards asked.

"Be there in time to," Ellis said. "A good enough place. Nice view."

"I wonder if I wouldn't like to ride on up there, an' have a look at the other side," Sisson said.

"It's the Platte, Andy," Ellis said. "The flattest thing you ever saw."

"How about that Fort Kearney we hear about?" Drew said. "We see it from the hills?"

"Don't know," Ellis said. "It's new to me."

"It ain't but hardly started," Piper put in, and pleased to do so. "They just put the money up last winter." There, goddamn it, he had them.

"Likely won't be much of it to see, then," Ellis said, and by his tone dismissed it.

The others passed it over, too, hardly giving it pause for thought, and Piper spat on the ground at his horse's feet.

Sisson fingered the reins in his hand, and stared ahead.

"By golly, I think I will ride up there. Anyone

comin'?"

"I'll go along," Gideon Drew said. "Sounds to me like God's outdone Himself up there. How about you, Ellis?"

Jim Ellis looked around, taking stock, before he answered. "All right. Emmet?"

"Sure enough. I wouldn't miss it; I see Davis comin', too, now."

"You joinin'?" Sisson said to Piper, and Piper wondered if the other man was trying to make it up to him for all the trouble he'd caused at Independence Crossing.

Then he thought, to hell with him, and with the others, too, and said, "No, I'll see it soon enough. I got no time for play, with all these folks to keep an eye on."

Feeling the importance of the words, he made a thing of necking his horse around; and then he saw the glance pass between Sisson and the pilot, and the knowing smile on Ellis's face.

They rode off, and Piper went back along the train. He saw some others join those going forward toward the dunes—Aaron Davis going by alone, and Thaddeus Morton, on one of them fancy thoroughbreds of his, riding in a group; altogether, there was quite a mess of them.

Well, let them go, he thought. Let the children have their games; he would stay here at his post like a wagon captain should, seeing that things went on like they was supposed to go. It was a good thing someone had a serious, grown-up mind, the way the rest of them was all behavin'. Supposin' a passel of Sioux should suddenly show up, what then?

He stared at the plodding livestock behind the train, restive now as they caught the smell of water from the Platte. A glint of something golden reflected sunlight in his eyes; he saw the brass knobs on the horns of Sisson's brindle ox which plodded with the loose stock. It bawled again.

Impulsively, without thought save rage, he moved in and seized the creature's tail; and wrenched it savagely, feeling pleasure in the act. The animal bellowed out its pain, and lurched ahead, gazing back at him with brown eyes showing hurt and lack of comprehension.

"Take that, you mustard-colored bastard," Piper said. "I only wished it was the one that owns you."

Up ahead, the voice of his querulous wife Nellie squalled loud and rasping above the turning of the wheels.

"Sit down, Jamie! 'Fore you bust your head! You'll see the river soon enough!"

It was a good day to go afoot for a spell, Esther Sisson thought. The air was warm, and lazy in a way, inviting you to idle some, or maybe snooze awhile, but at the same time hinting that you might miss something if you did. Full of spring, it was, and the earth, too, moist still from the deep rains, yet not so wet you got your shoes all muddy. In between, almost, on the pleasant side of dust and muck, both. The smell of it said you ought to put a crop in, quick. And they would, she and Andy, if they were still in Indiana.

She walked beside the lead span, her eyes on the riders growing small against the dunes. Andy still stuck up among them, big and lumpy, looking a size or two more than the horse could handle. Some men just weren't built to grace a horse, the thought came to her, the memory of twenty years seeing Andy without change in that respect. He'd been no different when she'd married him.

The thought lingered, and the warmth of memory chilled; the shadow of old grief, turned sharp of a sudden, and cast into bold relief now that she was dwelling on it. She was feeling moody today, with the Platte coming soon, with the turning west at last. Memories that lay just beneath the surface of the mind were coming out now, as though for a final look, like they would be left, too, with the hills and woods and deep-running rivers, far behind, forever.

She thought of the boy, dead four years; Jody, the young man who never was, the only child. Was it right that she and Andy should go away and leave him?

She forced her mind away from it, and became aware of Nancy Drew, whose appearance had gone unnoticed in the flood of sadness. The tall, angular woman walked with sure strides beside her, a bright eye taking the measure of the land about them.

"I saw you walkin', Esther, an' I thought I'd join you, if you didn't care."

"Why, I'm glad you did, Nancy. It's a nice day for walking, it seemed to me." Her thoughts came back slowly from the hill above the Wabash, the grass now growing rank about the marker. But she was glad for company, truly glad.

"That's what I thought, too," Nancy Drew said. "I got so fidgety, just sittin' in the wagon; an' Gideon's gone off with the men to see the river."

"My Andy went, too," Esther said. "Does your team pull alone?"

"Pretty well, but I put Tom, my oldest, to lookin' after it. Best to keep him busy, else he'd be foolin' around them Mabry girls all day. Not that they ain't nice enough, but he's young yet."

Her oldest, Esther thought; her oldest. Her mind stumbled on the richness the words implied, and then went on. The Mabrys, too, were blessed, even beyond the Drews, though to hear Susan talk sometimes, you'd never know it. But five, Esther thought; how the Lord had heaped his wealth on them.

Really, she must shake this melancholy mood. Her hand reached out and moved along the surface of the nigh ox's curving horn, thinking that Andy would be polishing them again, now that the mud was left behind, and the effect would be worth the effort.

Nancy Drew took note of the movement, saying, "Such pretty animals. And they seem to work so well together. Don't you have one with golden knobs on his horns?"

Esther smiled, pleased and proud that folks took notice of Andy's care and training of the oxen; that people looked on them with admiration.

"That's Star," Esther said. "Andy's got him in the livestock column today, for a rest. He's worked hard, especially at the crossin's."

"I seen him at the Big Blue, when he pulled the Pipers out. My Gideon said he never saw the like of such an ox."

"He is a special sort, at that," Esther said, still aflush with pleasure. "I guess he's our pet, you might say. Like one of the family, almost."

"Oxen get that way sometimes," Nancy Drew said. "Them, an' maybe a milk cow that a person's had a long while. It don't seem to me that a horse does, though, so much; maybe they don't strike a body as bein' quite so woman-gentle, or dependent on a person. Except for an old plow horse now an' then."

"Why, I do believe that's true," Esther said, understanding it, and at the same time feeling gratified to find she'd always felt pretty much the same.

"Come clear from Montpelier behind 'em, we did," Nancy Drew said, "except we rode a paddlewheel steamboat across the Lakes to Milwaukee, with our wagon wheels lashed in the riggin'. Even then, we had oxen pullin' us along the Erie Canal, from the Hudson River clean to Buffalo; barge men had a name for 'em—a 'horned breeze.' "

Nancy Drew laughed gently with the recollection. Vermont was a long way off, near as far as a body could imagine. The thought of a journey from there to here, and still beyond, was staggering to think about. Across the Lakes upon a snorting steamboat! Then the long cold weeks through Iowa, Wisconsin and a part of Missouri, too, until they came to Independence. And somewhere in the middle, a voyage behind a "horned breeze."

And they were hardly started on the worst of it. It gave one to wonder about the strength and spirit of the Drews. It moved one to give thanks for being of a party with them.

"There's a lot to come yet, it looks like," Nancy Drew said, as though their minds were going along together. "I guess we ain't seen but the smallest part of it."

"You seen more than we have, so far, but there's a sight more to go."

"In God's time, I guess we'll make it."

In God's time, Esther thought, and looked ahead. They were coming through the hills now, the way winding among the barren dunes, through the sparse grass, the prickly pear, the rutted sand. In a while she saw the men through a wide defile, on a point above the valley, standing beside their horses; standing, the strange thought came to her, like they would stand in church.

Then the wagons came through, the hills opened wide, and Esther saw the valley going west, the Platte winding blue and thread-like in the sun. But she couldn't comprehend what she was looking at, for the stunning vastness of it all. It came, then, with a rush, land so flat she couldn't think where the end of it might be, a sky so deep, so everlasting wide she couldn't think where even God might find a place in it. The whole of the West smashed full upon her in wild immensity, plains without limit, without end, mountains beyond measure in their height, beyond comparison in their savagery, a million buffalo thundering on the land; wild torrents, icy in descent, Indians stamping to their heathen drums, prairie wolves slinking through the grass.

A catch came to her throat, a sob, and the Wabash murmured under spring-soft skies. And on the hill, the grass grew thick about the solitary stone.

Good-bye, Jody boy, good-bye. The unvoiced cry was born of ceaseless anguish. Good-bye, good-bye forever.

FIVE

Davis waited off to one side of the breaking circle, with his arm raised, so the other men could make him out through the confusion of the wagons moving into line. His horse was blowing vapor like the others coming toward him—Drew's, then Morton's, and finally Emmet's, with the pair of pack mules trailing on the hackamores.

"How about it?" Davis said.

"Any time," Emmet said, and Drew and Morton nodded. The three of them sat scrunched and rigid in their saddles, their heads drawn into their shoulders against the early-morning cold.

"All right. Let's move."

Davis necked his horse around, and let it find its way among the gathering stock and random wagons. Near the grazing area, the others came abreast of him, and the soft sounds of the falling hoofs became prominent as the noises of the train receded.

Davis looked around him as they moved, aware of the day, his mind going out to the hills, and beyond to buffalo which they were to hunt. The sun was rising on their left, making long, hard shadows of the horses, and resting on the dunes and hills ahead, above the valley. The light lay on them golden-like, it seemed to him, sharp and clean with the new day, implying a warmth in contrast with the mist and dew-chill of the campground at dawn. The look of it somehow made him feel more conscious of the cold discomfort of the hour, of the feel of stiffened buckskin leggings against the goose pimples on his legs, of the way the beads of moisture overlaid things.

He'd be sweating a shirtful by the time they brought the buffalo in, but right now another can of coffee would go good.

They moved across the lowland meadows where the grass grew nigh to the bellies of the horses, where a wolf some times slunk off in plain sight, or an antelope paused in curiosity, its white throat shining in the sun.

"I seen a file of buffalo come to the river earlier," Gideon Drew said. "Be them, will it?"

Davis looked at him and was again aware of the spareness of the man, the lank face, the ends of the bones sharp and prominent. It was like he'd been put together with only the bare essentials, thrifty and saving of material. Even his voice was lean.

"If they're on top when we get there. Ellis don't want no huntin' in the valley, on account of stampede danger to the train."

"I presume we'll go through the hills, then," Thaddeus Morton said as he moved his horse in closer.

"Yeah," Davis said. "They always go back, anyway; only come down at dawn an' nightfall to drink."

"Do they always follow those trails?" Morton asked.

"Maybe not the same ones every time, but they

follow ’em, all right. They’re the easiest way of gettin’ down. We’ll likely take one our own selves.”

“I see. In which direction will we hunt, then?” Morton asked, like he was going to leave an address where he could be reached while he was gone.

“Where the buffalo are,” Emmet said, and Morton glanced sharply at him, but said nothing.

“Anywhere beyond the dunes,” Davis said then, “except where there’s a big herd. Mostly south, an’ west.”

“We’ll go along with the wagons, then, more or less, won’t we?” Morton said.

“Something like that, but south, more, likely.”

“And then cut back toward the river later on, to meet the wagons, I take it.”

“Uh huh. We’ll pick ’em up at the night corral, likely twelve, fifteen miles from where we stopped last night.”

“Well, well,” Morton said, as though it came over him like dawn. “I’m beginning to see it now. It’s like a triangle, then, we ride two legs, and the train rides the hypotenuse.”

“I’ll be goddamned,” Emmet Edwards said, and he stared with awe at Morton.

They rode on, Morton quiet now, and thank God for that, Davis was thinking to himself. It was too early in the day for talk, unless there was a need for it. It was enough to get your mind woke up, and your body working proper, without having to make a lot of conversation, too. Yet, you might know that Morton'd have to have the whole day lined out for him before they could hardly get a start.

Some folks, the thought went on, couldn't set one foot before the next without they had to have it all set down on a map exactly where that foot was going to light. Himself, now, he wouldn't burden his mind with all that detail. It was enough for him to know where the train was likely to be come night, and to figure on meeting up with it by dark; and in the meantime, to enjoy himself out here. How could a man figure how to get downwind of a buffalo if he forever had his eye on the sun, working out what time it was?

He was glad he wasn't that way. Emmet surely wasn't, and Drew neither, from what he could tell of him. Drew might be a dour, sparse-talkin' man, but that was nothin' to be held against him, and his eyes was aglint right now as he watched a herd of antelope skim across the ground half a mile away, and there was a smile, too, underneath that high, arched nose. He was pleased Drew had asked to come along; and maybe Morton wouldn't be so bad, once they got to hunting.

But why in hell did he have to start the day with triangles—an' worse, that other thing the wagon train was ridin' on?

When they came to the dunes there was a defile

winding to the prairie. The buffalo had made a deep and narrow trail here, and the horses followed it, single file. Trailing the other three, Davis looked back as they went around a shoulder overgrown with clumps of salt grass, and saw the wagon tops glinting in the sun, far away and down, strung out along the river, the oxen plodding forward, silent with the distance. The fourth day heading west, the thought occurred to him. And who could say how many more to come?

Then they came to the head of the ravine, and Davis saw the dark mass over the swells of land to the south, far off; like a great shadow cast by a cloud upon the tawny grass, or a piñon forest farther west. Knowing what it was brought a deep breath into him, and he tried to think how long it was since he had seen a sight like that.

"Buffalo," he said.

"God almighty," Drew said, with honest reverence.

"Let's get them," Morton said, as though the spectacle filled him with impatience. "What are we waiting for?"

"They ain't for us," Davis said. "Not them; too many in the bunch." He looked around again, and saw the scattered groups of smaller numbers, strung all the way from the hills to the dark mass on the horizon. "We'll take some of them trailers over there."

"Aren't we going to run the big herd?" Morton asked the question like he'd paid a dime and only got a nickel's worth.

"No point in it, with the easy meat over there," Davis said. "Once you get a big bunch runnin', you can't tell about 'em."

"Hell, man, they're miles from the train."

"They could get there fast if they took the notion. Anyway, meat that's been run hard afore killin' can give you sickness, too."

Morton let a snort out of himself. "I expected some exercise out of this hunt. I'd have stayed with the train, had I known it only amounted to stalking."

"You can run all the way back tonight, then," Davis said, irritated now, and wondering why Morton should gravel him more than other men. "Supposin' we split up," he said to Emmet. "Me an' Drew can circle right; you an' Morton left. We got the wind afore us. Better let us have a mule."

Emmet passed the hackamore to Davis. He and Drew were afoot now, standing at the head of the ravine.

"We leave the animals here?" Drew asked. "Looks like quite a ways over there."

"No. We'll lead them."

They headed out on foot, moving to the right of a swell of land which ridged southward from the dunes. The sun was higher now, and Davis felt the growing warmth of it upon his neck. Now that he was shed of Morton, he felt better, more expansive; he felt pleasure, thinking of the buffalo.

"Y'ought to see the bulls in August," he said of a sudden, for no reason, simply because the mood had struck him. "They fight like crazy."

"August?" Drew said, and added as he thought about it, "it must be the rut, then."

"Uh huh. An' beatin' each other to death, like."

Drew laughed, and Davis liked the sound of it. Drew was going to be a good one to have along for buffalo, given he could shoot. That old Harpers Ferry musket didn't look like much in that direction—wasn't up to a Hawken, by any means—but you couldn't tell too much from that. Sometimes, them as used them real old ones shot twice as good as the next man, to make up for the shortcomings of the gun. Being the kind he was, Drew'd likely had it since he was a kid, and'd no doubt keep it 'til the termites carried the stock away.

Beyond the saddle in the swell there lay a shallow bowl, with still another swell to the west of it. A deep ravine ran north and south through the middle of the hollow, and they had to turn to get around the head of it. The second swell was lower than the first, but broader, and from the top of it they saw the buffalo again, still far off, eating grass in isolated groups of cows and calves, with maybe a lone bull now and then, off by himself in solitary ugliness.

There was one more deep ravine, and a high swell rising from the farther wall, and when they crossed these, nothing lay between them and the grazing animals.

"They still got a quarter mile on us," Drew said. "Do we belly up on 'em?"

"No. We can walk within range. Seein' us don't mean much to 'em; they got poor eyes anyway. An' hearin' don't seem to scare 'em none either, 'less it's a thunderstorm or such."

"Scent, then, mostly, it sounds like."

"Uh huh. They get the smell of you, they're off. But the wind favors us."

"Pretty near in our faces," Drew said.

They started down the long slope toward the buffalo. Davis carried his rifle in the crook of his arm, aware of the pleasant feel of it, the nice heft, and the power implied by the hardness of the barrel. This, he sometimes thought, was the best part of hunting, this coming up to game, the sizing up, the planning of the shot, well-placed.

"You're loaded, ain't you?" he said. They were within a couple of hundred yards of a pair of cows, grazing off some distance from a larger group. A bull in a patched coat, still shedding, stared at them like an old man with a dark beard as they slanted off to go around him.

"I'm loaded," Drew said. "What about the bull, there?"

"He won't bother none. When we get around him,

he'll get our scent an' move."

They went another seventy yards or so, the bull beginning to snort and stir around as the smell of the men came down upon him. When they came to a halt, he glared at them with near-sighted eyes before he lumbered off.

"This is all right," Davis said. "Better take one quick, the bull's made 'em edgy."

Drew passed his bridle to Davis and raised the musket to his shoulder. The cows were something over a hundred yards away, restless now, not grazing any more, but watching as though they had it figured out that the old bull had something to do with what was going on. They were just beginning to sidle off when the shot came, and the smudge of powder smoke after it.

"Missed him, by jiminy!" Drew said.

"Look again," Davis said. "They're just slow goin' down, is all."

The cows had stopped by the time the second shot echoed off. The first one looked around, as though to find the source of it, but the second simply stared at the ground, rooted there it seemed like, until the knees began to give. It went all the way forward on the under part of its jaw, when the haunches broke down, and it rolled over on its side. Curious, but with alarm growing in her, the standing cow made a sniff at the fallen one, then swung around and broke into a heavy trot. Davis brought his own gun up, and sent a lung shot after it, the cow going down as the first one had, slow, in easy stages.

"By gum!" Drew said. "There's meat on the fire; let's cut 'em up."

"Load up first," Davis said, and the saying of it abruptly turned his mind back as something in his memory clicked in place. He remembered his first shot, a big bull on the banks of the far North Platte—no, a cow had not been good enough, not big enough. He saw the bull again, the biggest bull in the western plains, go down with the single shot, and as he ran toward it, abloat with pride, lunge up again, and charge; charge him, and Chabrun, too, and they both ran headlong for the river, with the bull's thunder in the ground and Chabrun's laughter in the air. He saw it just like yesterday, his hands fumbling with the horn and pouch, dropping the ramrod in the water, with the second shot bringing the animal down at last. And Chabrun knee-deep in the water, nigh convulsed in his amusement.

He was smiling now with the memory of it as they came to the cows and let the blood out of their throats, the warm smell of it thick in his nose. He made the throat incisions longer, to remove the tongues, and then he slit the hides along the spine to take the hump ribs out.

"We'll take the hams, too," he said.

"How about jerked meat?"

"Not enough time on the trail. Maybe we can kill a

few later on to jerk at Laramie, if we get to lay over for a few days."

"We have enough from these?"

"For now. Time we take the cuts from them, and a couple more, we'll be all right," Davis said. "The wolves'll take the rest."

With the wolves in his mind, he glanced up and saw the sharp muzzle and pointed ears partly hidden in the grass twenty or thirty yards away. "There's one now."

"Where?" Gideon Drew swerved around, found it, and brought his musket up, as if to shoot, and Davis laughed.

"You shoot him, his brother'll take his place. A man can't carry powder an' ball enough to burn 'em all down."

"Well, I'll be," Drew said, and after a moment, added, "there's another. They sure get the smell of it."

"Uh huh. In no time." Davis was working on the hams now, peeling the hide back from the heavy leg meat; remembering how Chabrun had always had a taste for marrow guts, and thinking that only the old-timers had been that way. He was aware of Drew moving through the fringe of his vision, turning as each new wolf caught his attention. Then Drew stopped, facing south.

"Somethin's comin'," he said.

Sioux, Davis thought, first off, then cussed himself for the notion. He got up from his knees, and found the rapid movement, far off, approaching them, the rider like a dark arrow skimming over the folds of land.

"Could be Emmet," he said. "Or Morton."

"I didn't hear no shootin' from that way," Drew said.

"We wouldn't. Pretty far off, an' the wind's wrong, anyway."

"Trouble, you think?"

"Hard to tell," Davis said, but already he knew it was.

The rider had seen them now, and was turning slightly in their direction. It was Emmet, Davis could tell that now, and he was riding fast over ground which was dangerous for speed. That much in itself meant something, it occurred to him; but Emmet's coming on alone meant more.

SIX

Thaddeus Morton waited until the young man named Emmet Edwards was well out from the ravine before he mounted his horse and headed farther into it. In a moment it opened into another, through which he rode a hundred yards or more, until the bank lowered and he could put the horse onto the prairie again. A swell now hid him from the other man, and when he came in sight of him again, Emmet Edwards had discovered his absence and was no longer working on the buffalo he had shot.

He was booting his horse northward toward the dunes.

Morton turned his own horse south, aswell with satisfaction. Be damned to him, he thought, and good riddance into the bargain. And similar sentiments to Davis, and to Ellis, too, tenfold. If a man had any pride he would be put upon for just so long. There had to be a line drawn somewhere.

He cared for none of them, the thought went on, now that he was dwelling on it; though the degree and nature of his dislike varied with each. Ellis he cordially detested, the mule tail being foremost in his mind whenever he thought of him. The pilot had made a fool of him that night, and Morton faced the fact for what it was. When others had done the same, on those exceedingly rare occasions in the past, those involved had always lived to regret it later on. One day Ellis's time would come.

Davis was a different matter altogether, something of an unknown quantity. He was Ellis's man, no doubt, but the worst that could be presently said of him was that he lacked respect. It was hard to put a finger on, that lack, but it was evident in his omission of deference to his betters; in the irritating, close-mouthed way he set about things—this hunt, as a case in point, without advising anyone of the procedure to be followed. Another thing—only the vaguest stirring of intuition—made him think it might be better all around if Molly had a child to care for; though the Lord knew he, himself, loathed the mewling brats like poison. But hadn't the wise old soldier said, on going off to war, "keep 'em pregnant, and take their shoes away"?

As for Edwards, he was an adolescent upstart, with too much wind in his voice for the brains behind it.

It made him feel better to be going off alone like this—a tacit denial of their implied authority, if nothing else. Riding with the train, or in the camp at night, he was always conscious of the primitive, yet highly specialized skills these three possessed, but already his present solitude was providing him a certain sense of isolation from them. They seemed to think that everyone who hadn't picked lice from his hair was a dolt who must be led through this strange, new country by the hand. Davis, in particular, it would seem, held himself solely competent to hunt in this environment.

He would like to see Davis riding to hounds with one of the Ohio River hunts sometimes; granted, of course, that his oafish presence be accepted in a company of gentlemen.

The theme broadened as he dwelt upon it, and he thought about the others. God, what a raggle-taggle lot! Sisson, making a fetish of those wretched oxen. And Isaac Piper—did he ever bathe himself?—his only saving grace his bending to suggestion. Providing you could stand the odor while you talked with him. And his wife, a shrew of the coarsest voice.

What on earth could creatures of such stripe hope to make of themselves in Oregon? They had not the wit to recognize an opportunity if they saw one, let alone exploit it. Born to the plow, at the plow they'd die; and never know what they had missed.

Which would only make it easier for himself. He could not complain.

His mood was improving by the moment now. Simply to be apart from the wagon people rather inclined him toward a feeling of paternal kindness for them. Boorish, yes, but sturdy, too, for the most part, and there would be need aplenty for brawn in Oregon, and on the trail as well, before they got there. Very likely, it was a good thing to have them as they were.

As though that settled everything, he dismissed the matter from his mind. He was now some miles from the point where he had left young Edwards. South still, but westerly as well, he saw the vast herd come in sight again, grazing and appearing motionless, but in reality slowly drifting west. They were still a long way off, and it occurred to him that distance was deceptive here, for they appeared to be no nearer now than when he'd started toward them.

Well, small difference that would make, and he raised the beautiful thoroughbred into an easy canter with his heels. This horse would get him there in no time if he was called upon to do so, and anyway, time was of no matter. Davis had given him the details, and he'd learned all he had to know; he had better than half a day in which to enjoy himself. Let the others stalk and creep; he and the thoroughbred would have a time of it.

He let the creature move faster now, aware of its eagerness, the reserve of power, strength which he had to quell rather than call upon. It was the first good run they'd had in a longer time than he could think of, and the horse was feeling the freedom much as he. Those endless miles of pacing with the wagons were galling to men and animals of mettle. It was a pity, Morton thought, that he could not have the other two out here running, too.

He guessed he was two thousand yards from the eastern fringe of the grazing buffalo. Two thousand, fifteen hundred, then a thousand. He would stay to the north of them, select a straggler, and run it west. If the rest of them took flight, likely they'd head south; Davis's fear of stampede was exaggerated, certainly. Still, the possibility existed, and he did not wish to be held responsible for starting something he could not finish. He did not wish to incur the peasants' ill-bred wrath again. One night of that had been enough. God-damn Ellis, anyway.

A thousand yards, five hundred, then a quarter of a mile. The horse was running splendidly, and now the sound of its approach began to arouse those buffalo which were nearest. An old bull, standing far out like a sentinel, looked up, and began to move, drifting toward the herd and breeding wariness among the others.

The alarm rippled inward rapidly, and suddenly Morton found himself among them. Humped backs heaved and stumbled into a run on either side; calves bawled for their mothers, and the cows bellowed in return. Swirls of dust kicked up as the pace increased. To his left, the main herd quickened the movement of its drift, sliding over the land like a flow of muddy water. Morton got the feel of it, the gathering of forces, the ponderous initial motion, thinking this was the way to do it; this made a man feel good to be alive. He would have his run; let the others hunt for meat.

The sound grew now. It seemed to have a physical quality, like thunder close and shaking, reverberating, rolling out and upward, as more of the animals were gathered into the tide.

He saw the great and shaggy bull then, running to his right, and up ahead. The main herd had commenced a slow and lumbering swing to the south, away from the source of fright, but the great bull ran alone and headlong toward the west.

Morton touched his heels to the thoroughbred's flanks and the animal surged, diminishing the distance, yet not so rapidly as he had thought it would. The speed of the bull was mildly surprising to appreciate—intoxicating, too, in that it sharpened his appetite for the chase.

Then they were alone, he and the horse with the tremendous bull, running over the swells and hollows, breaking through the steep ravines in clouds of dirt, the dust coating his face, and clods of suds flying from the buffalo's lathered coat.

He felt elation now, wild elation, sailing across the land; he felt the weeks of long monotony slide off. He felt a measure of his frustration go, of his impatience with men and women of little learning, little imagination, little grace. He could laugh at Davis now, and even Ellis.

He came beside the sweating, gasping bull and heard his pistol crack as he fired into it. He thumbed the hammer of the Patterson and fired again, and still again. He was aware of laughing as he slowly killed the animal, as the blood pumped out upon its hide, as the tongue protruded in drags of air.

Still the bull ran on, but now it swerved to gore the horse, and Morton had to grab the saddle to keep his seat. In his vast surprise he saw the blunt face and the wild eyes, and the curved horns black and battered, and fear thrilled through him on a sudden. He felt the sparkling, icy shock of knowing something had gone badly and inexplicably amiss, and then he felt the animals collide as the thoroughbred failed to clear itself.

He had the time for one more shot before the horse went down.

Morton lay on his back with the sky moving in great eddies, wondering if he was dead, and then he heard the horse screaming and knew he wasn't. He got up slowly and saw the two animals sprawled nearly together yards away, the great bull still at last, but the horse kicking its hind feet into the tangle of its own intestines. There was one ball remaining in the pistol, and when he put this into the horse's head the screaming stopped and everything was quiet.

When the stunning shock began to ease, he became aware of his loss, and felt the grief and sadness occasioned by it. He felt the rage, too, last, but superseding, gradually, the first emotions. Someone should have told him this could happen, the thought moved dully in his mind. Ellis, Davis, Edwards—any one of them, or all of them, should have told him this could happen. They should have told him what a weary, wounded bull would do.

He moved slowly toward the thoroughbred and knelt to remove the bridle, and then the saddle. But the remembrance of the living horse, vibrant in the sun, came over him, and then the warm and penetrating stench to which that shining life had been reduced, and he was sick, suddenly and violently. He heaved up to his feet and staggered off, trying to find the wind. He held his hands above his head, as though he might grasp it as it passed, and circled slowly, looking, too, like it possessed some physical quality he might put his eyes on.

Then he became aware of the appearance of the land, the strangeness of it, now that he was afoot instead of mounted. He tried to think how long the run had lasted, and could not. He tried to recall the look of the country, the shape and contours, but everything had changed. He had no idea where he was or how far he'd come.

A rise lifted to the left of him, and apprehensive now, he ran to it. From the top of this the view was much the same as down below, except that there was more of it to confuse him. He saw nothing he had seen before, no life or movement. Even the buffalo were gone, as though the earth had opened up and swallowed them. And the land rolled on forever.

At last he remembered the sun, and stared at it. A thin cloud had spread across the sky, but the sun was there, thank God for that. It was nearly overhead, slightly off the zenith; when he stood with his back to it, a short shadow was cast before him. Wouldn't that be north? If it was noon, it would be. It was worth a try.

He started off the rise, and a hollow rose around him. There was another rise, lower and to the right this time, but he had to keep his shadow straight ahead, so he ignored it. But as he looked that way he saw the gray-white shape move across the top of it, in the direction of the horse and bull. Rage and sadness filled him once again as he thought of what the wolf was going to do.

He went through the hollow, and over a low saddle, and into another depression. There was a rise beyond this, and then a bowl, quite deep, with a long and tiring slope on the other side. The hills and gullies ran into one another with a tiring monotony, and after a while he forgot to enumerate each as a feature in itself. The ground must be covered, and that was the end of it.

After an hour or two he remembered the sun again, and it occurred to him that he would have to correct his bearing for its movement to the west. The shadow was not so sharp and prominent any more, which meant the cloud was thickening, but it was longer, and there was still enough of it to go by. If he carried the shadow to his right a little, increasing the angle of it from his body every now and then, he could continue northward properly. And later on, there would be the buffalo trails to follow to the river.

Inch by tired inch, the shadow lengthened and became fainter, and the land rose and fell away from him. One time he saw the distant dunes from the crest of a higher than ordinary rise, and though he had been looking for them, they did not now excite him. He simply marked them off in his memory as a landmark seen and recognized. His mind was busy with other things, with the loss of the costly horse, with the anger occasioned by its death, with the conviction that Davis, and Ellis, too, were as much responsible for the disaster as he, himself.

By God, they should have told him, he thought again. Granted, he had asked to come along, and granted, too, he had slipped off on his own; still, they had been negligent and at fault for not advising him in full about the buffalo. Davis had led the party, but dimly as though he had been the guiding spirit, Ellis loomed as the symbol of the tragedy.

Now it was growing late, and the sky was dull. The cloud had erased the shadow altogether, but it did not matter because he could see the dunes quite plainly, even though they still looked far. He had been farther from the river than he had thought.

He did not think about the Indians until he was startled by the buffalo, which appeared quite suddenly, going toward the Platte as dusk came on. But even after he recognized them for what they were, the Indians, once suggested, became a fixture in his head, and gathering darkness acquired a sinister aspect because of it. Awakened now, his imagination saw Sioux or wandering Pawnees where common sense declared it was impossible for them to be; behind a clump of grass no bigger than a hat, in the person of a walking calf. Ellis had made a fool of him with the mule tail, but what he'd said on that occasion had awakened him to frightful possibilities, as well.

Then he heard the hoofbeats of the horse, approaching through the long ravine behind him, and his fears fanned up in sudden flame. He did not need to turn around to see the brutal, painted features, the glitter of the knife or tomahawk; or his bloody scalp fluttering at the pointed lance head.

Irrationality took hold of him, and he began to run. He was running through the deep ravine, running now and stumbling and getting up again and running on. Instinct commanded him to draw his pistol, but that only made the running worse, because he had not yet reloaded it, and now the powder ran like water from the flask, and the balls slipped through his fingers. Once he dropped the weapon, and when he stooped to pick it up he heard the hoofbeats very loud and close as the walls of the ravine trapped and held the sound. The implications of the nearness inspired bright new terror, and he discovered he was sobbing over his futility with the gun.

Then despair became a sort of resignation—despair and pride, and the humiliation of a coward's death—and he stopped and turned around, and saw the horseman looming in the dusk. He saw the dark bulk against the sky, and the clear line of the rifle across the saddlebow. A final, raging frenzy seized him as he thought of the imminence of death, or worse, and he threw his arm back to hurl the pistol, then froze in that position as he recognized the broad hat brim and the sound of the rider's voice.

"Davis!" Morton felt degraded and debased that Davis should see and hear his naked fright.

"Yeah, it's me, all right. Put that gun down, you damn fool."

And Morton stood there, staring at him, stunned. He was free, he was safe, he was alive, he would sleep beside his wife tonight, and go on again with the train tomorrow. But these things, while very real, were at the moment secondary to the astonishment he felt at his capacity for harboring both thankfulness and bitter loathing.

SEVEN

That crazy bastard must have thought you was a Sioux," Emmet Edwards said. "Runnin' off like that, an' then tryin' to brain you with the gun."

"I guess maybe he did," Davis said, seeing it again in his mind's eye, and seeing the shame, too, that followed the fear. "After he seen me, maybe he wished I was."

"Too bad about the horse," Andy Sisson said, as though the animal came ahead of its owner in his thoughts. "Them thoroughbreds are nice. Won't find another out this way."

"He's still got a mare and a stallion," Jim Ellis said without turning his eyes from the fire. "Give 'em time."

"Maybe he got a lesson out'n the business, anyway," Emmet said. "Be worth it if he did."

"That takes time, too," Ellis said.

Davis lay back against his saddle and let the talk move around and over him. He drank a swallow of buttermilk from the can he held, reflecting on how nice it was that a cow could fill a bucket in the morning and that the movement of a wagon through the warm day would provide a man such a refreshing drink come night. He was thinking, too, about the haze which lay across the stars like muslin, and wondering if that meant weather coming up. Distantly he heard the music someone played for the young folks dancing farther off. The oldest Drew boy was handing one of the Mabry girls around, and he felt a smile come on his face watching them; thinking now how dancing seemed to make a woman graceful and a girl again, and yet make a young girl somehow secretive and womanlike. He felt easy and contented with these thoughts; even Belle did not disturb them.

"You missed Rondeau an' some of his trappers today, Aaron."

Davis turned his head when he heard his name, and saw Ellis smiling at him.

"When'd he go by?"

"At the nooning. We was pulled up when we seen him comin' east."

"From Fort Laramie?"

"Uh huh. With hides. No more beaver."

"No more market neither. Hides, huh?"

"That's right. Buffalo. He had three, four wagons loaded. Too bad you wasn't there; he asked after you."

Davis gathered his knees in his arms, and looked into the fire. He saw Rondeau's black and bearded face, his bandy legs, shoulders that would pride an ox, the ancient shirt and leggings steeped in blood and grease.

He saw Rondeau drinking with Chabrun, and heard their tuneless singing.

Eh, qui est la belle Rose,
C'est le fils de l'heritant
Belle Rose—Rose et Blanc . . .

Or did it go like that? Much time had passed, and the songs had always been accompanied by alcohol.

"What about the trail ahead? Between here and Laramie?"

"It's all right. Plenty of grass, he said."

"Meat, too? What about meat?"

"There's meat. Between here an' the South Platte crossin' anyway, we got the pick of it. Some spotty beyond, to the Fort."

"Spotty?" Davis asked, and then because Ellis took time to select a brand to light his pipe, Davis had an intimation of the why of it.

"Them was the words," Ellis said through a screen of blown smoke. "But I always figure a Frenchy says more with his hands an' eyes."

Davis looked into his mind and saw Rondeau's eloquent hands, explaining about the buffalo; he saw the great herds going down before the hunters, the knives shining redly as the hides were taken, the bleaching skeletons arching their empty ribs upon the prairie. Speculating now, he saw the smoke-filled lodges where the shamans of the Sioux were inquiring of their manitous about it.

"Hides," he said, half to himself, "they're startin' on the buffalo."

"What do you mean?" The firelight accentuated Sisson's features and expression. "Trouble ahead?"

"No. No, nothin' like that." Ellis said it easy, and he chuckled around his pipe stem, but Davis had the notion he was making a play to pass it off.

"What do you mean, then?" Andy said, like he was pressing the point, seeking more assurance.

"Just the buffalo, is all," Davis said. "To some they're profit, to some they're life."

He got up then, and moved off into the tunnel of dark that lay between the small fire where the men were gathered and the larger one where the dancing was going on. The talk had made him restless of a sudden, though he couldn't say which part of it had been the more responsible—the reminder of what Rondeau represented, or the implications of the hunters going for buffalo instead of beaver. Either was unsettling of itself, the one stirring ashes of gone but still remembered fires, the other perhaps suggesting an altogether different sort of blaze.

He remembered again the thing he'd said, "to some they're life," and thought, detachedly, as though someone else had spoken, that the truth sometimes dwelt in the most casual of words.

He shrugged the mood away, walking toward the larger fire. They were mostly young ones dancing, but some of their elders were going at it, too, squaring off in sets while the fiddle squeed and the concertina gave the fuller melody.

It was late last night when m'lord come home,
Inquirin' of his lady,
'N the only answer he received,
She's gone with the Gypsy Davey.

He came to the fringe of light and stopped, wondering what he was doing there. The couples were either the very young, unmarried, or those who had already fought their battles and come to terms. There was no one in between, in that kind of twilight, like himself; no one married but yet alone. Still, the music had spoken to him, it seemed like, and he lingered.

Well, he hadn't rode 'til the midnight moon
'Til he saw the campfire gleamin'
An' he heard the gypsy's fiddle play
An' the voice of his lady singin'
The song of the Gypsy Davey.

His eyes became used to the change from light to dark to light again, and he saw other people shaping out of the shadows on the edge; people sitting on kegs and boxes, in groups or pairs, come to watch and listen. He passed them over, but returned his glance again to Isaac Piper, surprised at what he'd taken note of in the captain's face, the lechery, the outright animal desire.

Then he looked beyond and found Molly Morton outside the clear light on the other side, standing hesitant and shy, as though she might like to join the dancing but understood the impropriety of doing so without her husband; seeming the more alluring for her indecision.

Without a clear reason, Davis moved around the fire in her direction. He was thinking, wryly, that this was almost bound to happen some time, that it might as well be now. Isaac Piper's barren lust was amusing to behold, for all the fact that a man felt dirtied to look upon it; but it served to turn his own mind inward on itself, to make himself aware of what he harbored secretly. He wondered, by God, if he looked as all revealing as Piper did.

"I figured to ask about your husband." He spoke the lie, and knew she recognized it for what it was.

"He's been asleep for an hour," Molly Morton said, and her easy, knowing laugh made a joke of both the question and the answer. "You don't really care, do you?"

"He brought it on his own self, but he was in my party. He didn't have much to say after I caught up with him."

"Losing the horse was the worst of it," Molly Morton said. "Unless it was losing his pride, as well." She was speculating, he could tell, estimating him.

"A ridin' man goes afoot against his will, there's hell to pay," Davis said, and he didn't hesitate about the language because he sensed a kind of camaraderie between them.

"When he's like Thaddeus, there is. He didn't take to walking into camp before the eyes of everyone."

"He had a choice, but he wouldn't ride with me."

"That would have made it worse."

"Saved a lot of boot leather, though, it would have." They were bantering with one another now, and he knew she was enjoying it.

"That's the last thing he was thinking of. You learn a few things anyway about a man, living with him."

When she paused, he didn't say anything because it seemed like she was going to elaborate, but the music just then commenced again, and she was quiet for the moment, her attention on the dancers and one foot tapping to the sound. His eyes took in the lights and shadows of her face, the blood pulse in her neck.

"I'd like to dance," she said abruptly, watching the dancers still, and with her eyes set in a way that seemed not to see what was out before her, but something far away, in another place, much removed from this.

"So would I." They came on impulse, the words, and the movement of his hand to her arm, and she turned with a feel of it, a new thing in her face, an awareness of the intimacy implied.

Then she glanced down, her hands clasped primly together at her waist, as though consciously correcting the unguarded moment he had sensed.

"But we'd better not," she said. "I have to go to the wagon. It's getting late."

"I'll walk with you, then." He made a statement of it, not a question.

"All right." She was more restrained, and agreed without looking at him. "It's over that way."

When they turned away, Davis became aware of Piper's watching once again. The look, it made him feel sullied, still; but he could understand it.

The fire was behind them and he took her arm to guide her through the dark, becoming acutely conscious of her femininity as he felt her flesh soft and firm against his hand. They walked beside the wagons, the shapes looming dim and huge in the night, and the obscurity of everything made their walking intimate. There was sound, still, from the dancing they had left, but it was distant and remote and seemed to accentuate the silence which the physical closeness had imposed upon them. He could feel the pulse in her arm beneath his hand, and he thought of the life beat in her neck again.

When they came to a clutter of kegs and boxes which choked the way, Davis lifted her over. He put his hands around her waist and was surprised at the lightness of her, and at the hardness of her body, too, as he put her over and set her down again. She was like a boy, the thought came to him, in her being slim and lithe and supple.

The impulse took him and he stopped her as she began to walk again. He held her shoulder and turned her half around, and saw her eyes understanding it as he pulled her toward him and kissed her. She came easily into his arms, not eagerly but willingly, as though she had foreseen the circumstance and accepted it. He caught the clean, washed fragrance of her and thought of that and the heat and nearness of her as he pressed his lips down; and the life beating in her neck, and then the clean smell again which made his head swim.

Then she drew away from him, and stood with her forehead resting on his chest, her hands lying lightly on his shoulders. "This is awful." Her voice was small and weak. "This is terrible."

"Why?" Davis said. "What's wrong with it?"

"Isn't it obvious?"

"You don't love him. Admit it."

"Don't say that. You don't know."

"I can tell. I've watched you, and I know what he's like." He was feeling rough and angry now. Women always had to make a problem out of nothing.

They got started toward the wagons once again. This time he didn't take her arms, but the sense of intimacy still remained, implied by the pressing of the dark and by the remembrance of the embrace. But he knew she was trying to be impersonal now, contriving lightness in her mood.

"Is she beautiful?" she asked, like she'd put her mind to forgetting what had happened.

"Beautiful?" Davis said, although he knew what she was referring to. "Who?"

"Your wife." She said it slowly, with good humor, as though she had caught him at something, and was being sly and mildly reproving about it. "Were you going to keep that from me?"

"No," he said; he was aware that she was smiling in the dark, and he wondered where she'd learned about him. "Of course not. I'd of told you."

"Well, then?"

"Well, what?" He was on the defensive now, and neither liked it nor understood how it had come about.

"Is she beautiful?"

"Yes, I think so. But what has that got to do with it?"

"And you love her, don't you?"

"Sometimes. I don't know. I don't think so."

He was mad clear through, and he turned her around again. He grabbed her arm and pulled her roughly and crushed her against him with his arms around her and his hands behind her shoulders. When he kissed her she was relaxed and unresponsive first, until the fierceness and the feeling that was in him seemed to go to her, and then she pressed against him and kissed him hard, then warm and soft. When her arms came from around his neck and she moved away, she didn't pause to look at him again but turned and walked to the wagon down the line. Davis watched her until she went inside the arch of canvas; then he stared blankly at the pile of buffalo chips he was idly kicking. He wondered who had ever had the energy to gather a quantity so immense.

EIGHT

Well, summer was here, it seemed like, Andy Sisson thought, walking beside his oxen as the wagons lined out behind the pilot. Leastwise, the last few mornings had been warmer than those before, if that meant anything; making it easier to roll out, to get the camp struck, to get the train moving out again. Nothing like a dew chill to make a person slow to set about things.

He nosed the air, taking in a breath of it, and letting go of it again, slow. It was warm, all right, and scented, too, with the wild flowers and the grasses blooming out. Still, it might be early yet to make anything certain of it, and there did seem to be a kind of weight to it, sultry-like, almost, even if there wasn't a cloud to be seen just then. It was a queer land, though, and a man had to know the signs before he could be sure of anything. If he was back in Indiana he'd know if the warmth was here to stay or not.

The thought of the old place turned in his mind, and he stole a side look at Esther, walking beside him for a spell. It was a sad thing she took this moving on so hard, but he was glad to see her out and walking some these past few weeks, and not staying in the wagon as she'd done before, simply staring out.

"You ain't overdoin' it, are you, girl?" he said as she turned her head and caught his look.

"Doesn't feel like it," she said. "I'd rather walk, anyway, than set all day."

"The time passes quicker, that's sure," Andy said. "It kind of drags on this stretch, anyway, everything bein' so much the same every day. Be a change, though, soon."

"Change? Where?"

"When we cross the South Platte, Ellis says. We go through Ash Hollow and on by Courthouse and Chimney Rocks and Scott's Bluff. It's different then. All bent-like, an' heaved up an' twisted."

"A change for the worse, then," Esther said, but not bitterly. "Just gets wilder and wilder."

"It's wild, all right," Andy said. "But great, too, in a way. It makes you feel full of power and daring just to think you're goin' through it. It makes you want to see it all, every last acre, don't it?"

"I'll allow you the daring part of it," Esther said, and now he saw the smile on her lips, the patience she would have with him whenever he was behaving out of character. Then the smile went away and she looked ahead again, as though her thoughts were going farther on along the thing he'd said.

"Is it like this all the way, Andy, do you know? And out there, too?"

"In Oregon?" Andy said. "Like this?"

"Empty, I mean, and big. So big you feel lost, and almost naked. Aren't there any little valleys out there, with groves of trees, and meadows; where it's friendly toward a person, instead of overpowering?"

It was a woman's question, a question from a lonesome woman, from one who'd lost her only child, who was barren now and far away from everything she'd ever known. But who was staunch and uncomplaining, who asked little beyond assurance now and then. Andy felt a catch come into his chest, and a wave of tenderness went out to her.

"We'll find such a valley," he said, and he was surprised at the sound of his own voice, at the edge of determination on it. "We'll find a valley that's got everything." Then he saw the shadow move across her face, and he knew no valley in the world would have everything for her again.

The turn of the talk had made a mood and they were quiet for a time. A rasping caught his ear and it occurred to him that he'd have to tar the axles once again. The air was drier now, and warmer, too, and they didn't stay greased up so well. The trail going more to dust every day the way it was didn't help things either. The oxen's hoofs would need attention, too, again. There was always something needed looking after, but then life wouldn't have much use of a person if there wasn't.

He reached over and tugged on the yoke, seeing if it was fitting still. Somehow that yoke didn't seem to be just right on any animals save Star and Bill, his mate, for whom it had been made. He half-wished he had Star leading out today so long as he was spending all this time afoot beside the team; he was good company, even if he was an ox. But in another couple days, so Ellis said, there would be the South Platte to be gotten over, and Star would be making good use of the rest he was getting now.

The South Platte, he thought, and his mind lingered on the words, as though he'd spoken them aloud. The South Platte and the bent and broken land that lay behind it toward the North Platte.

With a deep, deep ache, he wished he had his boy, his Jody, walking here beside him.

The nooning came, and some of the men gathered for a smoke when the eating was finished. Andy walked over to Ellis, Drew, Piper and some of the others who were lighting up their pipes and taking their ease in the shade of the wagons. There seemed to be something in the west holding their attention as Andy joined them.

"Looks like smoke," he heard Gideon Drew remark, and he saw the faint smear across the far sky for the first time.

"Might be the Indians set the grass afire," Edgar Mabry said, as though his mind flew to the worst interpretation first thing. "They do that to help the new growth, don't they, Ellis?"

"Now an' then," the pilot said, with scarce a look from the filling of his pipe. "But they ain't today. I vote for rain."

"It does look like cloud, at that." Andy spoke for the first time, and Ellis looked up at him from where he sat.

"You feel it in your bones, Andy?"

"The air feels thick, somehow," Andy said. "I wasn't sayin' nothin', though."

"A cautious son, ain't you?" Ellis said, and then went on. "It's a cloud, all right. We're due for rain." He poked his finger into the bowl to set the coals, and took a long look into the west. "Some of these can get pretty active."

"All right to move through it?" Mabry asked the question of no one in particular, but just as though the thought had simply popped into his head.

"If it's goin' to blow, we best stay in corral 'til it's done with." Isaac Piper made something of a statement of it, and Andy figured he might have read it in that guidebook he spoke so much about.

"Can't get much wetter on the move," Ellis said. It was more of a casual remark than a criticism of Piper, but Andy saw a vinegar look come to the captain's face.

"Holdin' back might delay us crossin' over the river," Drew said, and the others turned this over in their heads before any more was said.

Then a man named Henry Smithers said, "We figure on gettin' to the river tomorrow sometime, don't we? In time to cross the next day?"

"That's right," Ellis said. "It'll take a day to cross over."

"Ought to keep on movin', then, today, so as to reach the river in time for a good night's sleep," Drew said, and most of them nodded or grunted their agreement with this, except Piper, who seemed to feel he could not agree to anything without first having disagreed.

"Well, what about the stock? Ain't they liable to spook?"

"Might," Ellis said. "But no more'n if they're held; less likely to, I'd say. They don't get so moody when they're moving on."

Piper gave up his stand then, satisfied that he had taken every care to make his presence felt, and the talk went ahead to the river again. Only half-listening, Andy looked to the west and watched the clouds piling up now, spreading north and south. In the far southwest, he saw movement coming through the dunes and thought, buffalo, but changed his mind when he remembered the hour. As the specks became clearer he recognized Davis and Edwards coming in, early on account of rain perhaps, and the wish came sudden that he could join them on a hunt sometime, that he could feel free to leave Esther by herself for a day.

When he heard his name, he turned around, aware that he was being spoken to.

"About the river, Andy," Ellis was saying to him, "seems we ought to work out a kind of order in goin' over."

"Like who should go where and when?" Andy said, and he was wondering why Ellis had used his name to bring this up before them.

"That's it," Ellis said, and though he was speaking to them all, Andy held onto the thought that the pilot had alerted him for something special. "It can be a risky business, an' the more we plan in advance, the easier it'll go."

"I expect I ought to call a meeting of the council," Isaac Piper said, as though the matter should be discussed in private first.

"Sure, if you want to," Ellis said. "I just thought I'd mention it."

"I think maybe I'll call one for tonight," Piper said, more definite, like the idea had put its roots down deep.

"No reason why you shouldn't," Ellis said. "Thing you want to keep in mind is havin' some good man an' team lead off, so's he can serve as a mark for the other animals to strike for, and follow after."

"How's that?" Piper said; it was plain he hadn't come across that in the guidebook.

"Animals get in a swift current as wide as the Platte, they sometimes lose their heads an' sense of direction. A steady team that goes across first can keep the line straight, an' once there can wait in the shallow as a mark, if need be."

Andy shuffled his feet when he felt Ellis's eyes move around to him. He had the growing notion that the pilot had been talking of him, and at the same time he wondered if he wasn't being vain and big-headed to fit himself into the description Ellis specified. Then the pilot grinned, and Andy knew that it was so.

"Maybe you ought to think of tryin' it," Ellis said to him.

"I never forded a river that size before," Andy said. "We rafted the Muddy."

"None of us have, save Ellis here," Drew put in.

"Well, there's plenty of time to think about it," Piper said, as though it was a small matter, after all, and hardly worth the time for talking of just now. "We'll take it up along with the rest of it when the council meets."

"Sure," Ellis said. "A good idea."

"Time to hitch up," Piper said, as if he had already put the matter from his mind. He made a show of scowling at his pocket watch, but Andy saw a glance that had remembrance in it slide his way.

The rest were getting up, tapping their pipes against their hands, tugging at their trousers. Ellis swung up to the saddle of his horse, and moved away so the wagon men could see to guide on him.

Andy gathered in his oxen, and brought them to the wagon, where he hitched them up. He felt a swell of pride, of bigness, suddenly, and it likely showed, for Esther watched him with a somehow knowing smile.

"What were they talking of?" she asked him.

"Talkin' of? Oh, not much, just about the river comin' up." He fastened the last of the trace chains, wondering if he was passing it off as he'd intended, but thinking not. He'd never learned to hide his feelings from her. "Ellis spoke me up to lead across the river."

"Why, Andy, that's an honor. I'm proud of you."

"He was thinkin' of the oxen, likely. He knows Star can't be beat."

"Yes, he must have been. That Star could do it all alone." She spoke with faint mockery, her smile becoming wider.

"I don't think Piper liked it," Andy said, and the glance, bright with animosity, came to mind again.

"Oh, him! He didn't volunteer to lead, himself, I'd bet."

"No. He didn't. I guess he just likes to come up with them ideas his own self. He's called a meeting for tonight, to talk about it."

"But, they won't change it, will they? The lead, I mean?"

"No, I don't guess they will," Andy said, and now that he was thinking of it, he was sure they wouldn't. Piper'd like to, sure enough, but Ellis's word had weight, for all the fact he was only "hired help," as Morton and Piper were pleased to call him. Ellis had aired his opinion before a gathering, ahead of any meeting, and so his views were well-known in advance. He'd done it just right, the thought occurred to Andy, easylike, in ordinary talk, as if he'd planned it that way. The council'd had a taste of what it meant to go against the group.

Then the call came down the line, "Roll 'em! Roll them wagons! Get 'em movin'!" and the oxen pawed, the axles creaked, the chains rattled on the lurching wagons. Andy's lead span lunged into the yoke as he shouted at them and touched them lightly with the goad. The dust rose from the trail.

The wagons were moving now, and Andy looked ahead.

"It's goin' to rain," he said.

"Rain? Why, the sun is shining, Andy."

"I know, but Ellis said it would." He turned around and smiled at her, feeling the pleasure and the pride again, and feeling grateful, too, that she was pleased as well. It was good to see her happy, if only for a while. He wished he could do things all the time that would make her smile.

"Then, I guess it will," Esther said, her face full and pretty with the lifting of her lips. "My respect for what he thinks is growing."

NINE

Isaac Piper went down to his wagon to tell his wife Nellie about the rain before he began to patrol the line. He didn't much care whether Nellie got wet or not, but the canvas should be laced across the openings, on account of wind; else it might tear loose and the whole business get soaked right down to the rind. Money was short enough without havin' to lay out for new flour an' such come Fort Laramie; an' two, three times what you'd pay at Independence, too.

"What's wrong?" she asked straight off, as though his coming to the wagon once the train was under way meant there had to be trouble of some kind. She sat on the seat, looking out at him like a wary turkey, her neck red and corrugated, eyes sharp and intent, shadowed by the bonnet.

"It's goin' to rain," he said, and he was aware of being careful not to say that Ellis had told him that. "Them clouds over west're comin' fast."

"I seen 'em," Nellie said. "Are we goin' on?"

"Why not? We'll be off on our timin' at the river crossin' if we lay here 'til it's over." It never paid to tell her of his disagreements and differences of opinion. She always used them against him later on. A sharp tongue, she had, and quick to belittle with it.

Nellie shrugged. Piper thought of the turkey once again, wondering if the Morton woman popping in and out of his mind so much had anything to do with it. Her and Davis going off together; by God, he'd remember that.

"All right," Nellie said then, "you better give me a hand with the canvas."

"Let the kid do it. I got work to do." Piper shifted around in his saddle, and looked up and down the line, businesslike.

"That's right. The captain don't do no handwork no more," Nellie said. "I clean forgot."

"That ain't got nothin' to do with it. I got a hundred people an' more to see to right now." She always picked the damnedest times to run him down. "Jamie!" he shouted.

The boy's head appeared beside Nellie, his eyes big and dark in the white face. He was still sickly, somehow, despite the sun. And his nose was running.

"Help your ma with them lacin's," Piper said when the boy did not ask what he wanted.

"Can't I ride with you, Pa?" Jamie asked. "You said I could some day."

"Well, this ain't it, kid. I got a lot to do. It's goin' to rain here, in a while. You help your ma."

"The captain's a real busy man, Jamie," Nellie said. "He ain't got time for us when he's busy bein' busy."

"You better hurry," Piper said, and he ignored both the tone and meaning of what she'd said. "Wind be comin' soon."

When she didn't say anything, or didn't move to leave the seat, he thought to ride off, but changed his mind. He'd best tell her about Sisson and the river. She'd hear it somewhere anyway, and he might as well tell it as he saw it.

"We talked to Sisson 'bout leadin' off across the South Platte," he said. "He's got the oxen for it."

"Sisson?" Nellie said, and right away he knew what was going through her mind. "I thought the captain led the way."

"I said he had the oxen for it. Everybody knows that. As much as I want to, he's still got the oxen; an' we decided."

"All right, Isaac, don't get in such a stew."

"I ain't in no stew. I'm just tellin' you how it is."

"I know. You don't have to make a show around me." She was smiling at him now, maliciously. "Sisson's got the oxen. Forget it."

"That's right, he's got the oxen."

"He's got a big old black mule, too, ain't he?"

"Goddamn it," Piper said. "Go to hell."

He necked the horse over and rode forty-fifty yards at an angle to the trail, and got down to water out. To hell with them, he told himself; everybody done it, an' God help the one that tried to hold it in. If they didn't know by now they never would. It was a lot of fancy foolishness makin' like it was only done by animals, then bein' conspicuous by hidin' out behind a wagon, or gettin' a ring of other folks around you, like the women sometimes done.

He felt mean and he didn't give a damn. They was all against him now, and he didn't give a damn. In his sly way, Ellis had made a mockery of the council, wheedling a decision from the crowd before a matter ever come up for talk an' judgment. But Ellis was only a part of it, and not the biggest, either.

He got back on his horse and rode along the line. The sky was overcast by now, and rain was coming sure. It was coming even though he might not care to think it was, but Ellis had been right, and now it was. A drop fell, splat on the back of his hand, and made a dark mark in the powder of dust upon it. A gust of wind raced along the ground in front of him, and he put his head down as it swept around him and away.

They were tying down against the blow. All along the line they were lacing covers, lashing gear, and taking such things inside as might be spoiled by wetting. The men who would be out were turning up their collars and putting coats on. Horses that weren't being ridden at the moment were being tied behind the wagons. He saw Morton bring his pair of thoroughbreds up and fix their hackamores to the tailgate of his wagon, and he thought again how Morton was kind of keeping to himself ever since he'd come walking in. The horses had their blankets on, and though he'd seen them rigged out in those before, he'd never got used to the sight of them. Red, by God, as bright as sunset.

The sight of Morton and the horses made him think of the woman, and of Davis going off with her beyond the fire. He was filled with rage again at the thought of the hunter daring what he hadn't been able to bring himself to do. And then he felt the lust in him get the better of the rage as he imagined what might have happened out there in the dark, and saw himself in place of Davis. Maybe he should have told Morton what he'd seen, but something had restrained him. Never tell when he might get the chance himself sometime.

The rain was coming regularly now, and the wind was growing. He buttoned his homespun coat and turned up the collar. Oddly, he felt good getting drenched and blown this way, though he couldn't say exactly why, except that it was a misery and discomfort they all must bear, not he alone. Yet it went beyond that, too, in a way he didn't understand; it made him feel defiant, somehow powerful and brutal, as though he was one and the same with the storm itself, detached and isolated from the people in the wagons, enjoying the battering they were getting.

It was a thought that appealed to his frame of mind,

and he let it run with him. He was alone now, that was it, alone in the midst of the crowd; ignored by those who'd chosen him to lead, ridiculed by his wife, though that was nothing new.

The disgruntled train captain saw the livestock following after the wagons, and the few men guarding them, their heads pulled into their shoulders, faces averted from the wind. The rain was coming down in flat sheets, wetting things over of a sudden so that they shone and glistened.

When he saw Sisson's brindle ox plodding with the herd, he thought again how everything bad and wrong commenced with it, somehow, and he remembered how he'd wrenched its tail, and wondered now why he hadn't pulled the damn thing off. The creature was symbolic of every insult, every slight, every humbling of himself. He was not good enough to lead across the river, even did he wish to risk the holes and quicksand first; but the brindle was. He was not the captain any more; the brindle was.

The brindle ox would show them the way to Oregon.

It was more than a man could bear. It was more than a man could stomach and keep respect. He rode up beside the animal in the gray, descending rain, thinking how he'd like to slit its throat. It was like the first time as he leaned and grasped the tail, but different, too, because he held it now with both hands, and slammed his heels into his horse's flanks, and kept holding until he felt something break or tear inside the great patient beast. The sudden jerk on his arms nearly pulled him from the saddle.

Then he heard the brindle bellow, and at the same time the world went blank, then dazzling in its brilliance as the bolt of lightning ripped across the sky. It was as if life and motion left everything on earth for just that moment of shattering concussion. He saw the wagon tops shine with an unearthly light against the black clouds. Everything stood out sharp and well-defined, as if he were looking through a glass. The earth jarred and shook with the vibration and the roar of thunder. He smelled sulphur in the air.

When he saw the brindle ox turning with its head down, he felt cold and loose inside. A second had skipped over in time and the animals were abruptly running east. His own horse reared on its hind legs as he jerked the bit and kicked his heels in. Everything went slow and clear as he tried to ride with the tide of maddened stock. Then his horse slipped in the mud, turned and began to fall. It speeded up again and as he fell he saw the wet backs and the hooves lifting up and punching down. When he struck the ground he opened his mouth to scream, but nothing came. He saw the brass knobs bright and shining on the curving horns. The stock ran on.

Andy put the tip of the shovel into the mud, and cupped

his hands over the end of the long handle, which came to a level with his breastbone. He felt conspicuous and self-conscious standing with it in his hands, like he might be thought to be in a hurry with the burying, but he wasn't the only one, and there didn't seem to be anything else to do with it. He'd simply have to hold it like this until Drew was finished with the reading.

The Lord is my shepherd; I shall not want.
He maketh me to lie down in green pastures:
He leadeth me beside the still waters.

Drew's voice came through the rain, and Andy heard the words of the Twenty-Third Psalm. He looked down at the formless shape rolled into the blanket and thought again of the livestock running and the lightning scorching through the sky and himself leaping on his horse and riding out to try and make them turn. He remembered the frenzy in the Star ox's eyes, the queer bend to the tail and the run of blood where it fastened to the backbone; and he marveled at it yet.

He restoreth my soul: He leadeth me in the
paths of righteousness for his name's sake.

He stared at the black hole of the grave, at the rain falling steadily into the darkness of it, and the rivulets spilling over the edge. He tried to see Isaac Piper alive again, but the sight of him ground into the mud, the scraps of clothing and the flesh dominated his mind and he couldn't drive it out. He wondered if he felt sadness or compassion or what, and then discovered he felt guilt because he couldn't tell. He wondered if he would have thought differently of Piper had he known that this was going to happen, but he knew that he would not.

Yea, though I walk through the valley of the shadow of death, I will fear no evil: for thou art with me; thy rod and thy staff they comfort me.

He became aware of Ellis standing across the opening from him. The pilot was holding one of the ropes with which the lowering would be made. Water dripped from his mustache, from his hat brim, and fell away from the taut rope in beads as he put his weight against it. Ellis's face was staring and transfixed as though he was far away, and the thought came into Andy's head that Ellis must have seen this many times before, in circumstances more harrowing than this, in places more outlandish. He wondered if those other, past occasions were living in the pilot's mind again; if he felt a part of himself go into a grave whenever a man was buried.

He could hear the quavering sobs of Nellie Piper now. She stood with Nancy Drew and Esther, her head bowed down upon her chest, barely erect, it seemed, except for the women holding her. She'd hated and scorned her husband, if the eyes and ears were to be believed, but she must have loved him in her own way, too. Or had the thought of going on alone already engulfed her? A man was good for something, however wanting he might be found.

Surely goodness and mercy shall follow me all the days of my life: and I will dwell in the house of the Lord for ever.

Andy saw Ellis let the rope slide slowly through his hands. The other three payed out at the same time and the one-time train captain Isaac Piper descended with the rain. Andy waited until the women had taken Nellie away before he moved the shovel—less brutal, somehow, it seemed. Then he dipped the wet blade into the mud and poised it over the hole, waiting for Drew to finish.

From dust thou camest,
to dust returneth.

He turned the shovel over and the sodden dirt slid off. Drew closed the Bible and put it in his pocket before he picked up another shovel. Ellis and Davis and Emmet Edwards were already digging into the low mound at the side of the grave, the rhythm of the falling earth heavy and uneven in its sound. With the five of them, it did not take long, and nobody spoke until the earth rose out of the hole, and they were finished.

"We'll run the wagons over it," Ellis said then. "Too wet to burn powder."

"The rain'll kill the scent, won't it?" Drew asked.

"Ought to," Ellis said. "If it keeps up. Can't do nothin' if it don't."

"Christ, I'd like a drink," Emmet said. The young man jabbed his shovel into the mud and tipped his hat back, as though the digging had made him overheated.

"I got some medicine in my plunder," Ellis said. "It'll do to take the chill off 'fore we start again."

"We ain't goin' to make much today," Drew said. "Should we stay here?"

"Best to push on," Andy said, and he looked at Ellis to see how it sat with him. He was wondering how it would be if he was Nellie Piper and had to spend the night with the place of death and burial just outside her wagon.

"Might as well go on," Ellis said. "We'll make something. You folks'll need a new captain now."

"That's right," Mabry said. He had just come up and looked from one man to the other. "Maybe we better have a general meeting of some kind tonight, for an election."

"I guess we better," Drew said.

Everyone was quiet for a moment as though Mabry's words had turned up old ground again, and they were thinking of it. Andy saw Ellis tug his hat and look around, like he was trying to put the thing together as it had happened.

"I'd like to know what made 'em run," the pilot said.

"That lightnin' was awful close," Drew said. "I could even smell it."

"They sure touched off quick," Ellis went on. "A good thing they run the way they did, else they might of got the teams agoin', too."

"Funny they should run the way they did," Mabry said.

"No accountin' for animals sometimes," Andy said. He liked animals, but he knew them, too. "Likely, we'll never know."

"Well, let's get that drink, then," Emmet Edwards said, and Andy knew the youth in him was pushing death away.

He looked at the low mound, at the slope of ground going into the mother-earth already from the rain, and thought of the wagons rolling over one by one. He thought of gunpowder that wouldn't burn, and of wolves and Indians that might come by. The Indians would discover they had no use for what they found below, but the wolves would make no never-mind about it. Meat was meat to them.

"Are you comin', Andy?" It was Davis who spoke,

and Andy looked up, aware that they were shoving off.

"You go along," he said. "I want to see my wife."

He couldn't think exactly why he said that, but it must have expressed a need of which he hadn't been consciously aware. Piper's dying must have something to do with it, as though it underscored the impermanence of them all upon this earth, upon this trail. It could have happened to any one of them, the thought came swift and clear, in that or any other manner. Whatever it was, it made him wish for Esther's company just then.

When he came to Isaac Piper's wagon he heard the hopeless sobbing above the rain, and he knew that Esther was still in there with Nellie and Nancy Drew. He stood there wondering if he should have come at all, half of a mind to join the other men, when he became aware of the pinched face looking up at him from beneath the wagon. He saw the large eyes and the shape of a child wrapped into the canvas tarp.

"You're gettin' wet under there, ain't you, son?" Andy said, and he knew he was talking to Jamie Piper.

"My pa was kilt," the boy said. The boy's eyes were fixed on Andy's face without expression.

"I know," Andy said, and he knelt down so their heads would be level with one another. "And I'm sorry; I surely am." He said it earnestly, aware of the sincerity of feeling.

"My pa was kilt," the boy said again, and it slowly

came to Andy that he was in a daze. He wondered if he'd been hiding out beneath the wagon all the time, throughout the burial and everything. A familiar, but long unfelt, compassion took hold of him.

"Does your ma know you're under here?" he said, but as soon as he asked it he knew she didn't. Even though the child didn't answer him, he knew. Nellie didn't know anything just now.

Then a new thought went on from that one, so natural it seemed to him that he spoke before he'd reasoned on it. "How'd you like to spend some time with us, Jamie? Your ma might like to rest a bit."

Andy waited, and when the boy said nothing he reached out and touched his shoulder. Feeling no resistance, he slowly gathered the boy into his arms, tarp and all, and stood up. As he turned to go, Esther let herself over the tailgate to the ground.

"Andy!" She saw him right away, and looked at him with surprise.

"I found him under the wagon. I wondered if we ought to take him for a while; maybe until Laramie."

Esther pulled the tarp back from the boy's face, and touched his forehead with her hand. "He's got a fever, Andy. He needs dry things on, and warmth. Of course, we'll take him."

"It'll help some, anyway," Andy said. "How's Nellie?"

"Busted up. She's going to ride with the Drews

awhile. Nancy'll send a couple of her boys to take the wagon."

Esther was talking fast and automatically, and looking at the child all the while she spoke. She was looking at the boy and feeling his head and neck, and his clothes to see how wet he was. She was being just like she used to be when Jody was alive.

"That's good," Andy said, as he thought about it.

They were walking toward the wagon through the rain and mud. He was aware of the weight of the child, and of Esther, fussing still, beside him. She was speaking of dry clothes again, and blankets, and wishing there could be a fire to heat water for a bath, and Andy had the queer thought that it was not so very long at all since he'd heard it all before.

"He should have a hot bath, Andy," Esther said again.

"I know. We'll have to wait, though."

"If the rain stops tonight, I'll give him one."

"All right. It may be late, though; we're going on."

"We are? How far?"

"I don't know. A few miles, anyway. Here we are."

They came to the wagon and Andy held the boy until Esther climbed in. Then he passed him up to her.

"I'll get him under the blankets right away," she said. "We can speak to Nellie about dry clothes later on."

"All right," Andy said. He stood for a moment

watching her, and he knew she'd forgotten him already, but he didn't mind. "I'd better hitch up," he added as an afterthought. "They're gettin' set to move."

He could still hear Esther talking soft and anxiously to Jamie as he walked away, and he wondered if it was indecent of him to enjoy the sound of it, to take pleasure in his spirit. He wondered if it was right of him to enjoy the feel of the child as a burden in his arms. He walked past the grave of Isaac Piper, hoping it was not a sin.

Then he heard someone shout, "Ketch up! Ketch up!" and his mind came away and went ahead. He was thinking of the team now, of hitching up, of whether he should change or not. The Star ox came to mind again as he thought about the livestock running, and he frowned at remembrance of the bent and bloody tail. It was a hard thing to explain no matter how a man might look upon it.

Had Star been hit in the ass by lightning?

TEN

The South Platte, Ash Hollow, the rusty sandstone cliffs and stunted conifers at Windlass Hill, the big rocks, Courthouse and Chimney, the North Platte, and Scott's Bluff still beyond; the sun rising every day, reaching out across the hard blue sky, and the wagons rumbling after it through the sea of dust, ever onward, ever west.

They were getting there, all right, the thought came time and again to Ellis. Though it sometimes seemed they were hardly more than a line of ants crawling upon the face of the wide and endless land, they were getting on with it. There might be a day going through the hills, where there was change and novelty, and an idea of distance covered given by the variety of scene; then there'd be another when they could look back from the night camp, and just about see the whole day's journey, and they'd know they hadn't come but another dozen miles or more. But they were getting on with it.

The South Platte was far behind now, but Ellis could hear still, as he'd heard before, the sand-filled water sawing at the spokes. He could see the wheelers disappear beneath the water at the bank as the wagons' weight came down upon them, then rise again as the leaders found their footing and pulled ahead; the wide loop of animals and wagons going over, drifting downstream with the current, lurching in and out of holes, and bending toward the far bank at an angle to the force of flowing water. The crossing had been easier than a lot he'd seen, come to think of it. They'd followed Andy pretty well. No quicksand sucked anybody down, the wagons all stayed upright, and nary an animal was lost. It was one of those times when thinking of it all the way from Independence had been worse than doing it.

The river could be bad when it took the mood, but

there was good to be gotten of it, too. You mightn't think so to see the women shake their heads over all the goods that must be dried, the boxes and barrels that must be packed again, the clothing that must be hung before the evening fires. And doin' it alone, the most of them; a man didn't somehow think he was a man when faced with woman's work. It was a revelation to see what one of them could think of to keep away from it.

But the wagons were tighter now, and that meant something. The dry air of the high plains, and the hot sun day on day, made for loose joints, made the spokes rattle and the iron tires wobbly on the felloes. An overhaul at Laramie would set them right again, but the wetting would help to hold them in the meantime.

So the South Platte was gone, and Windlass Hill, with the wagons lowering, one by one, along the steep slope, the rope unreeling from the axle of a wagon that was held, the end lifted so the wheels were free, the oxen arching their backs to hold the weight from running over them, the rear wheels chained to brake the long descent.

Then Ash Hollow with its canyons and its chasms, and the way so narrow the oxen rolled their eyes at the emptiness that opened up aside the trail, the men walking careful with their goads held ready, the women held into themselves and quiet, looking straight ahead as though that might make the canyons go away, the children gathered 'round them in the wagons, peering through the openings in the canvas, but quiet, too.

And the North Platte winding down below, small as nothing in the vastness of its valley, the shadows of its cliffs and ridges; the prairie dogs upright on their blunt rear ends as the wagons passed, the black and white of the magpies a flash of contrast against the earth shades of the valley floor, the russet layers of the rim; the antelope, spooked, but pausing, too, before they breezed away, now and then a buffalo grazing in the bottoms; the sky a million colors in the west when the sun went down, the sound of wolves and coyotes howling in the night; the black-eyed Susans, and the budding roses.

And now the big rocks, giant landmarks of the trail; different from any they'd ever seen before, breeding mystery and closeness in a man's heart. Like voices speaking of the strangeness yet to come, of the oldness, of the newness, of the size and distance that a man could never measure and make sense of, but only wonder at.

"That Chimney Rock," Gideon Drew had said, when first they came in sight of it, near a day away. "How big is it?"

"I never heard." And Ellis had wondered how much time had passed since he had ceased to fit this country into limitations. Miles didn't mean much here, nor feet, nor acres, but a man had to learn that for himself. "The Lord only knows, I guess."

"Could be He is the only one," Drew had said, as

though he'd understood, or sensed it, anyway.

It'd be a proper piece of knowledge for Him to have, Ellis had considered more than once since then. If there was a Lord, the kind that people like to think of, liked to speak to, He would know about it. He would have to, He had made it. Yet, accepting that, it only made the mystery deeper, the answer more obscure. Granted that there was a God who had made this land, had heaped it up like this, and burned it over, twisted it, and caused granite peaks to rise, and laid it out with grass, and scoured it with rivers, a land at once beckoning and repellent, there was still the why of it, the reason of it.

It made Ellis wonder if, unaware of the urge to know, he'd spent his life seeking.

There was a time when Ellis felt anger with the people coming in the way they were. There was a time when he felt the land belonged to him, to the other hunters and mountain men, to the Indians and to the animals that lived upon the timbered slopes beyond, along the streams and rivers notching through the hills, and on the plains and airy mesas. He held the contempt of youth, and of discovery, for anyone who might come trailing after, once the land had opened up and lost its newness.

Ellis saw, though, that change could come upon the face of a changeless land. He saw that beaver couldn't last forever, that rendezvous would peter out, that young men aged and turned to other jobs, or drifted off, or the law of averages caught up with them, that a dying breed would never be replaced, that red men became embittered, that one day the bucket would find no water in the well.

He saw these things, and thought that if you read the sign and understood, you could adjust to the changing times. You could if the land meant something more to you than beaver in the creeks, more than riot and whiskey at the rendezvous—then broke again—more than young squaws copper-skinned and willing while the night breeze whispered in the pine and aspen. You could if you were married to the greatness of the land, to the mystery of it. If first and always, until your final breath was drawn, you sought the everlasting why of it.

These days along the North Platte, creeping past the rocks, Ellis's mind dwelt more and more upon the old things, and there was another why to answer. He must be getting older than he thought, and in the way of ageing folks, moving backward in his mind to youthful pleasures in a younger day. Still, he had no particular longing to see those days again; he looked at them in retrospect, as the passing of a pageant through the land, of which he'd been, and was, an unknown but privileged player.

He was a guide now, and guiding wasn't so bad. It kept him in the country he was meant for. And since he no longer held resentment for the emigrants moving on to California, to Oregon, or to that place the Mormons were calling Deseret, he took a measure of amusement in their company, and derived a sense of usefulness in taking them where they had in mind to go.

One bunch was a good deal like another, experience had taught him; people were of all sorts, all tempers and turns of mind. He no longer marveled at the contents of their wagons, at the notions they might have about the country lying out ahead of them, at the reasons they might have for going where they were.

This outfit, as a case. On the whole, it was pretty much like others he had taken over. Riding out the long day, a part of him dozing, while still another kept alert, or sitting easy about a fire in the evening, his mind would sometimes wander over them.

They were getting pretty good, now, it seemed to him; better, certainly, with Piper gone. Looking at it one way, Piper'd done them all a favor by getting rubbed out when he did. His wife would have a time of it in Oregon, but she wasn't doing badly with the Drews right now, and that boy of hers was thriving with the Sissons. You'd think a newly widowed woman would want her kid beside her every minute, but it seemed to suit her that Andy and his wife should have the care of him a while. And it surely didn't look like they was bothered by it.

The mood seemed more settled, too, likely due in part to the memory of Piper's going, but more, he thought, to Andy's taking over as the captain. Andy'd stepped right into it and kind of pulled them all together. He was easy with them, an asker, not a teller, a kind of steady plodder who worked things out and didn't shy away from questions when in doubt. He had a kind of dogged courage, but he was careful, too; and he had those oxen.

Queer how folks came to estimate a man by the animals he kept. But natural, too, when animals took such a part in a person's life.

Himself, now, he didn't much care one way or the other about them. They were a means of breaking ground if you were farming, a means to pull a wagon, or to ride on, if you were going somewhere. In the old days in the mountains they were sometimes more of a hindrance than a help; they would wander off, they now and then made noise when you wanted quiet, and they drew Indians like meat draws flies.

It was different some, now that he was riding out across the country day on day, but even so, a horse, at least, was still a horse to him. He'd rather trade with the Nez Perces for a spotted Appaloosa that he could keep or not, as he saw fit, than make an agony of every minute owning one as costly as them that Morton had. A man had animals like that, he'd never get his mind away from them; the less he had in tow, the less he had to worry over. Ellis always felt it go against his grain to be a slave to "things."

Morton was a strange one, a square peg, that didn't

somehow seem to fit into a movement of this kind. Not a farmer, nor a man close to known and basic things, like the rest of them, but something different. Someone who responded to different drives, outside Ellis's own range of experience with people, and he suspected him. Granted, his stupidity on the buffalo hunt with Davis looked to have slowed him down, he still remained unknown and unpredictable. An odd man, any way you chose to look at him, made somehow more so by them fancy horses and a wife too young for him.

Now there was something; Ellis's mood would mellow when he thought of her. Could he shed twenty years, he might be right in there aside of Davis, playing up to her in the shadows of an evening; or even pile up buffalo chips for her cooking fires, like Emmet was doing on the sly. A queer way to a woman's heart, that struck him—or whatever it was Emmet was trying to get to—but you couldn't always tell. Women sometimes had more variety than men. One thing, though—a strip of flannel or a string of beads wouldn't do for her; Molly Morton was no squaw.

Davis the hunter, now, something ailed that one. He was like a man coming and going, both, and not knowing which he wanted. Trying to find his old life on the trail, yet seeing, too, that it didn't somehow sit with him, as though he wondered in the back of his thoughts if it was right to leave his wife as he had done. Trying to tell himself it didn't matter, and playing up to the

Morton woman as though to show the asking voice inside him that he didn't give a damn. A man who'd left the trail should let the memories lie, hadn't ought to try and pick them up again, especially one who'd set his roots down, who'd got himself a woman. A woman had it in her power to do strange and peculiar things with a man sometimes; but memories, if he tried to follow them, could do it, too.

But he could be dispassionate about Davis, about any of them—interested and amused, but not involved. He could even be dispassionate about himself. Life was short, a man came this way but once, and he could not go on forever. Someday, somewhere, Ellis knew his time would come, as it came to every man. He didn't much care beyond that simple fact; so long as it was in this land, he didn't care about the nature of it.

It was a good way to be, he sometimes thought, in a country so filled with possibilities.

It might have been the talk with Rondeau weeks ago that made Ellis wonder now. You could look for three things along the Platte—dust and mosquitoes and now and then a gathering of lodges, where the Indians came to trade along the river. Sometimes, when the shallow wells they dug went bad, you'd find fever breakin' out, but you surely didn't look for it. So far, they'd been lucky when it came to sickness.

But now they were going along the North Platte, and

Davis was telling him the buffalo were gone, and Rondeau was in his mind again because they'd come upon no Indians encamped. Maybe he was building up a lot of notions in his head, but a village somewhere along the water would be a reassuring thing to see. Even those Minnesota Sioux, all smeared in skunk oil, would be a welcome sight. He could abide the stink, just for the knowing they were there.

"We seen plenty of sign, Jim," Davis was saying again, and Ellis pulled his mind away from Rondeau and the Minnesota Sioux. "It's old, though, all old."

"Indian sign?" Ellis said. The sky was red and gold along the cliffs and buttes, and turning purple overhead and to the east. Far away, a day in back of them, Chimney Rock rose up to catch the last of the evening light. It was burning scarlet, like a torch, as if it had a secret, radiant life inside it, and he remembered his talk with Gideon Drew about it.

"Didn't see any," Davis said. "But a whole damned prairie full of buffalo bones. A lot been killed lately."

"Hide-hunters, likely," Ellis said. "Rondeau was right about that."

"We figured the same," Davis said. "Only saw but one alive, an' that a bull. We brought him in, though; couldn't be fussy 'bout it."

"We was pretty far south, too," Emmet Edwards said. The younger man squatted on his haunches with a can of coffee in his hand, his face made red and still more youthful by the fire.

"Five miles, anyway." Davis stopped in the middle of it, as though retracing in his mind the way they'd gone through the country. "I wasn't thinkin' of the meat so much."

Ellis felt Andy Sisson's look fall on him as the meaning of Davis's words took shape.

"Does that mean Indians?" Andy asked him.

"Might," Ellis said. "Hard to say, but it might."

"We ain't seen no villages yet, like you said we should. Could they be drivin' the buffalo away?"

"I don't know, Andy. Maybe." Ellis was being careful how he put it. Andy would be thinking of the kids, the women and the train, the days of driving before they came to Laramie. "But it don't mean nothin' if they are."

"Just that we eat salt meat awhile again, is all," Davis said, like he took the cue from the quiet way that Ellis put it.

"If they run the buffalo in deep, it's account of the hide men, ain't it?" Andy said, holding the trail of the first thought. "The ones that Rondeau feller told about?"

"Yuh, it could be," Ellis said. "They might be worried 'bout their food supply."

Andy Sisson hunkered down and let a stream of trail dust trickle through his fingers, and Ellis wondered if that helped him get things straighter in his mind.

“Do we need the meat?” he asked after a moment, looking up. “We got plenty of salt meat, speakin’ for ourselves.”

“So’ve we,” Drew put in. “I guess most have. It’s tiresome stuff to eat, though.”

“Nice to have when the fresh gives out,” Ellis said. He looked around now, aware of the growing size of the gathering. It seemed to him that a general uneasiness had caught them all, and he wondered why it was that the smell of trouble had a way of moving around so fast.

“Maybe this is one of them times, then,” Sisson said, still letting the dust slip through his fingers, still trying, Ellis thought, to avoid the idea of something coming up. “Maybe we ought to live on salt awhile.”

Davis shrugged, as though, being the hunter, it made no never-mind to him. “Whatever you say. Me an’ Emmet figured to jerk some buffalo come the layover at Laramie; it don’t make no difference, though, if we can get by without it.”

“What right do the Indians have to all of it?” Thaddeus Morton spoke for the first time, and everyone turned to look at him, as if surprised to hear from him again.

“None, I guess,” Ellis said, feeling that Morton had asked it of him. “First come, first served. But if they’re drivin’ the buffalo away, it means they don’t want no one else to have ’em.”

"Then we better keep away from 'em, for now, anyway."

Andy made a definite statement of it, and stood up. "Be more later on, likely, should we really need it. How about it, Jim?"

"Ain't much sense in stirrin' anything up," Ellis said, and he was aware from the look of Andy's face that he had said the right thing. It was too bad Andy had to buck a turn like this so soon after taking over, but he was glad it wasn't Piper trying to decide on what to do.

"I don't think we should let them know we're afraid of them." Morton made it clear he disapproved of the whole idea.

"No one said we were," Andy said, turning on him. "We just ain't askin' trouble, is all."

Ellis took a drag on his pipe, and moved into the pause when Andy stopped.

"Could be this is all about nothin'," he said. "Maybe Aaron, here, an' Emmet, ought to take another look."

"We thought to go to hell an' gone in tomorrow," Davis said. "We're bound to find somethin' if we go deep enough."

"That about settles it, then, don't it?" Ellis said. It was the best way, let it hang awhile.

"I guess it does," Andy said. He looked around, as if he expected Morton might have more to say. "It suits me."

Ellis turned away, then, making the first move to

break it up. Maybe Morton was putting another argument together, but his setting things in motion got the others heading off. By the time he poured himself a can of coffee only the hunters and Andy Sisson were by the fire, even Morton going, likely thinking he couldn't say much to impress the ones that stayed.

"Have a can, Andy?" Ellis said. "Here."

"Thanks," Andy said, then paused with it halfway to his mouth, as though a thought had stopped the movement of his hand. "Them bones, they mean hide-hunters, sure, don't they?"

"Uh huh," Ellis said. His mind was only half on Andy now, on the anxiety he knew the captain felt. His eyes were following Morton's blocky figure through the darkness closing in. Goddamn, it looked like Morton had got his second wind.

ELEVEN

The air was still, and the hoofbeats of the horses were the only continuing sound for as far as could be heard. Away to the north, the breezes from the valley would still be stirring through the broken faces of the cliffs and ridges where the plain began, but nothing moved out here. Prairie dogs slumped beside their holes as the horses passed them. Little owl-like birds stood motionless beneath the flimsy shade of sagebrush, their eyes closed against the hard light. Now and then a gray snake lay coiled upon itself in the shadow of a rock. The buffalo bones glared and glistened, and seemed to swell almost, as the power of the sun sucked the moisture from them.

"Damn, it's hot," Emmet Edwards said.

"Be thankful you ain't chewin' dust along the river," Aaron Davis said.

"I am, but it's still hot. I never thought it got like this so far north; it ain't even July yet."

"It does, an' it ain't near to bein' over with. Lots of heat to come with summer just beginnin'."

"Cooler in the hills?"

"Some. In the mountains, it is. Mostly, though, it's still hot by day. Wait'll we hit the Snake River plain."

"You sound like it's a damned desert."

"There's a lot of desert out there. Still, it ain't so bad as what they get on the way to California."

"The Humboldt Sink?"

"Uh huh."

"I heard of it. There's one down south must be like that."

"Down south?" Davis turned his eyes on Emmet, thinking again how much a kid he seemed, and thinking, too, how the impression was deceiving; how he was a kid, and not a kid, both.

"New Mexico. It's an old Spanish trail, part of the Camino Real to Santa Fe from old Mexico. Ninety miles of no water, no grass, no anything but sand and heat. Jornada del Muerto, they call it."

"Christ," Davis said, trying to imagine it. "What does that mean?"

"Journey of death. I guess they dug a grave every hundred yards in the old days, when the carretas came up from Chihuahua."

"You been over it?"

"Once, as far as Paso del Norte an' back. It was a bitch, all right."

Emmet was looking ahead as though he could see the desolation of the Jornada del Muerto spreading wide upon the Nebraska plains, and Davis wondered if he had laughed and cracked his jokes for the ninety miles of no water, no grass, and a grave every hundred yards.

"It makes you wonder, don't it?" Emmet said after the pause.

"Wonder?" He was still seeing Emmet drag across the ninety miles.

"Why they do it. Why folks are always heading off somewheres. Why they don't stay put where they are. Why they're always yondering, trying to see what's in back of beyond. I still don't know how why I crossed the Jornada, an' I ain't sure why I'm goin' to Oregon."

"Folks just get the urge, I guess," Davis said, and here was another side of Emmet, that he hadn't seen; figure him, speakin' out in riddles. Emmet had his smile on now, as he looked at him again, as if he knew he'd said something surprising, and not to be expected.

"Why're you goin', Aaron?"

" 'Cause the grass is greener, maybe."

It was a lame reply, and he smiled to make a joke of it, but the question still stood out sharp and prominent in his mind, wanting a better answer than what he gave. Why, it kept on asking. Why?

He thought of Belle, then. She was always in his consciousness; he could hold her far back, on the edge of it, but when certain things were said, or thought of, she came forward in his mind, unbidden.

Sometimes she was striking and alluring, soft and yielding in his arms, her fragrance fresh with promise like the breath of spring. More often she was ablaze with anger, raking him with scorn, saying she'd be damned if she'd leave the home she'd finally got, to take the trail to Oregon; saying she'd waited long enough for him to quit his roving in the first place, let alone putting up with more of it, and joining him to boot. Saying she should have learned the lesson from her old man—himself a footloose wanderer—and never tried to settle down with one like him. In the next moment smothering him with love, playing on him the way she knew so well, arousing his desires; then laughing at him, taunting him with mockery. Love and hate, tears and laughter, wild abandon, cold restraint. Her nature knew more moods than there were colors in the rainbow.

And she'd stayed. When it came to that, she'd watched him go with hurt and sadness, yet with fight left in her, too. Maybe the principle of the thing had overgrown the point of argument by then, but neither one had given in. And she had stayed.

What was there in a man that made him do the things he did? What was there in a man that made him throw his home up, and leave his woman, and take to a trail he knew had changed beyond what he remembered?

Maybe it was the people crowding into Independence, and the look of them—the ignorance, the innocence, but the don't-give-a-damn about them, too. Part, likely, the clutter and the hurry in the wagon shops, the harness shops, the tires glowing on the anvils, the smell of old Muddy in the spring, bringing silt from the Gallitan and Yellowstone.

A man couldn't buy himself a drink without he heard the talk on every hand; without there was another company making up beneath his nose, a captain being decided on, a pilot being chosen. He couldn't walk through the mired streets without he saw a leather-faced hunter cat-footing aside a furrow-stumbling farmer never beyond the Ohio River until now. Without he had to step out for a team of oxen pulling through to the camps beyond the town; or a newly bought span of mules, and the driver hardly knowing a jerk line from a nose bag. But the driver was going westward just the same.

It was like Emmet said, the thought occurred to him. They were yondering, going onward, following the sun, following something in their hearts and minds, the way a wild goose follows that which makes it fly when and where it does. A lot of them would break themselves before they got where they were heading for, and some would never live to see beyond the mountains, but they were going.

He knew he was no farmer seeking more and better land; he was different than the most of these new ones setting out. He was not a wild goose either. Yet something pulled upon him, too, something pulled him west again. The old trails were gone to grass, and a new day was coming on the land. He didn't understand the why of what he did, but he was going anyway.

Davis was ahead of Emmet going up the rise, and when he came to the point of topping out he saw the Indians far off in the shaking heat of the swale beyond, and he jerked the mare around to get below the level of the crest again.

"Indians," he said. He was on the ground already, winding the reins about a point of rock.

"How far?" Emmet was down now, too, tying to the rock, shifting his rifle in his hand, hitching his powder horn around in back.

"Half a mile, maybe less. Looked to be seven or eight of 'em." He was going up the rise again, hunching low, and Emmet followed him.

He spread flat before he reached the top, and bellied down upon the hot ground, the sharp, small stones. He inched up, pulling with his elbows and driving with his feet jabbed into the earth behind him. There was buffalo grass and stone and a clump of withered sage at the crest, and when he got behind this he could see the swale beyond, and the Indians riding at a slant, northwest.

"There they are," he said. "Could be makin' for the river."

"I'll be damned. It looks that way. Sioux?"

"From here, they are. Teton Sioux, my money says."

"Christ," Emmet said, his way with it giving out he knew about the Teton Sioux. "Is this bunch with the buffalo?"

"Part of the crowd, likely. Seven men for eight horses, though. Must have had trouble somewhere."

"Maybe one got downed in a run. There's another, there, looks hurt. An' the horse that ain't bein' ridden, too. Hip-shot, or something, looks like."

"Uh huh. That's what made me think of it."

They were closer now and Davis saw them clearer. The seven braves rode at a walk, the eighth horse strung on a line behind the last in the file. The led horse went with a limp and the rider on the one ahead of it sat in a queer, hunched-up way. They all looked worn out, and when he saw the paint he knew it was more than running with the buffalo.

"They had a scrap," he said, sure of it. "They got paint on, sure as hell is hot."

"I see it now." Emmet was lying pressed against the ground with his rifle out where he could use it if the need arose. "With the Pawnees, do you think?"

"Must be. Likely connected with 'em down by the buffalo, an' got jumped."

"Ain't often Pawnees can do that to Sioux."

"Must of hit a crowd, with only time enough to daub a little paint on; take a crowd to make Sioux look as sorry as these. They're likely hoppin' mad an' boilin' at both ends."

"If they're makin' for the river, how about the train?"

"Keepin' this heading, they'll get there 'fore dark, givin' they got a mind to."

"They're a hell of a long ways out. You think they know about the wagons?"

"Hell, yes; they know what's goin' through the country." Davis stopped and took a long look before he spoke again. The Sioux were going straight northwest; they hadn't changed since they'd come in sight. "They're comin' in, all right."

"I suppose we better pass the word." Emmet half-rose from his belly, then he made a grin at Davis. "Is there goin' to be a fuss?" he asked, and the way the words came out made Davis think that Emmet wouldn't mind it if there was.

"Ain't enough of 'em for big trouble. They'll likely ask pay for their poor showin' against the Pawnees. An Indian gets beat up, he's got to make face out'n it somehow; that's why these are comin' in, I'd bet. A pipe, maybe, an' some trade goods, ought to make 'em feel better."

" 'Less they ain't got the sense of full-grown warriors yet. 'Less they're young bucks still tryin' to build themselves some character." Emmet's smile was hard and bright, and Davis thought again how he had been around more than he looked.

"Yeah," Davis said, thinking of it. "That may be why they got in trouble in the first place." He squinted into the fierce, reflected light cast up by the earth and grass, and the heat waves turned and he could almost see the spring shoots greening and the travois going by again, the sun coming bright and clean through the rain-washed sky.

"Uh huh, Emmet," Davis said, half in thought to himself. "The Big Blue's a long way off."

TWELVE

Ellis had the wagons turning before they reached him. From the rimrock, Davis gave the signal, and the circle had begun to build by the time he and Emmet stretched out across the valley floor. The river lay flat and pallid, barely showing through the pall of rising dust, and the Big Blue crossing came to his mind again. Out here you forted up before you started asking questions.

Now, coming up to Ellis, the thought struck him that the pilot had been looking for this, expecting it, perhaps, or something like it; was likely relieved that the missing camps along the Platte were being explained.

"Trouble?" he said straight off, as the hunters reined in to ride beside him.

"Don't look too much like it," Davis said. "They're Tetons, though, seven braves, eight mounts; but one of each been hurt. We figure they been scrappin' with the Pawnees. They got paint."

"Looks like everybody wants them buffalo." Ellis took his hat off and ran his hand over the graying, sweat-soaked hair beneath. "Young, was they?"

"Hell, yes," Emmet said. "Looked full of fire an' beans, an' all in heat 'cause they got pushed around."

"Be in an askin' mood, then," Ellis said. "Time of day, they'll likely want to spend the night, too. Tell you what, we better stage a smoke an' make a thing of it."

Andy Sisson had come up in the middle of it, and Davis gave him the whole thing, from the start.

"Damn, I been afraid of this ever since we seen that Rondeau." Andy was looking at the rim as though he thought the whole Sioux Nation might top out any minute. "I don't suppose there's anything to stew about, though."

"There ain't," Ellis said. "And it wouldn't do no good if there was."

The circle had about closed now. Except for the fastening of the trace chains, the corral was made. The four men swung their horses off to one side, and got down, squatting on the ground where there was dust to poke at to help them think and talk.

"The same ones that run the buffalo away, too, I expect," Andy said, looking from Davis to Ellis, and back to Davis again.

"Likely some of 'em," the pilot said. "An' took time off for a brush with the Pawnees." Ellis raised his head and took a long look at the way the circle lay, at the bluffs lifting bright and scalding in the sun, and the river winding on. "This ain't such a bad place; we could stage a fight here if we had to. Better get the boys to hold the stock between the river and the circle. Be close, then, for night, an' we can turn them out in the early morning for a graze."

"What about the Sioux?" Andy asked, his mind still on them.

"We'll camp 'em off down river some. Keep an eye on 'em then. This smoke, I guess we better have the council for it. Suit you, Andy?"

"Be best, I guess. Maybe Aaron and Emmet, here, ought to sit in, too."

"That's good enough." Ellis took another look around before he spoke to Davis. "You want to round

’em up, Aaron?”

“All right. They join on you? The Sioux ought to show in half an hour, anyway.” Davis rose up, ready to mount again.

“Tell ’em to meet outside the circle. Ten, fifteen minutes ought to give ’em time enough. I’ll be out here where they can see me.”

“All right. I’ll pass the word.” Davis swung on up and the mare minced, like it had the smell of action coming up.

“I just thought of something,” Ellis said, and held him with his raised hand. “I don’t like that limping horse. They may want a trade, an’ them thoroughbreds of Morton’s look attractive. You might tell him it’d be smart to dust ’em over, so they don’t look like much.”

“I’ll tell him. He ain’t goin’ to like it, though.”

“Can’t help that. Rather argue with him than with the Sioux.”

“Goddamn, I forgot about him,” Andy said. “I’d like to keep him out’n it somehow.”

“So’d I,” Ellis said. He stood up and slapped the dust from his leggings, the action putting an end to the talk. “But we got to live with him.”

They began to move off, then, and Davis rode along the outside of the circle, an eye peeled for the wagons he was looking for. The dust was thick and heavy, still, because the stock was being moved, and the wagons had just stopped. The men were riding here and there, gathering to talk among themselves, or standing ready with their rifles in their hands. The women were staying in or near the wagons, mostly, trying to keep the young ones in control, knowing something was coming up, but not yet sure exactly what it might amount to.

Folks kept calling to him as he went along.

"What's up, Davis?"

"Trouble comin'?"

"They wearin' paint?"

He nodded and grinned and waved. No time to talk to everyone. He didn't stop except where he had planned to, at the wagons of the council members—Drew's, and Mabry's, and finally, farther down, at Morton's. No one was on the wagon seat when he pulled up.

"He's putting the oxen into the herd," the girl-voice answered from inside, and when her face showed in the opening he saw the color flash through it as she recognized him.

"Oh." It came in a breath and he knew her thoughts had darted back to the moment of reluctant ecstasy; perhaps not wanting to think of it, but doing so despite herself.

"It's me, all right. Ellis wants your husband for a smoke." He saw the blood pulse in her neck again, the hair metallic in the sun. It pleased him that she should be confused to see him—liking it, yet not wanting to, both.

"A smoke?" She took her eyes away from him, concentrating on the wagons across the way, as though the sight of them helped to keep her mind away from him.

"There's Sioux comin' in, an' we're going to talk with them." Beautiful, by God, she was, night or day; he remembered it again, the press of her against him, the red lips crushed and moist against his face. He was aware of smiling, thinking of it.

"Sioux?" She still looked out, she still tried to keep her thoughts, her eyes, herself, away from him. "I wondered why we stopped. Will there be a fight?"

"Nothin' like that. There ain't but half a dozen."

"Half a dozen what?" the new voice said, and there was Morton coming around the wagon, giving each of them a quick look as if he suspected them of something.

"Sioux," Davis said. He tugged at his hat and kept his eyes away from Molly Morton. "Ellis wants the council for a pipe with 'em."

"A pipe?" Morton said, and Davis knew that Morton would never think of anything like that himself. He'd have his own ways of dealing with the Indians.

"We got to treat these kind of careful," Davis heard himself say, and at once despised himself for feeling he had to explain it to him, the way he was. It seemed to say that he accepted Morton as someone special. "They're Tetons, an' they don't give a damn for anything. A smoke an' a few trinkets, an' we'll be clear of them."

"Are those the same ones than ran the buffalo away?" Morton wanted to know.

"Likely. It don't make no difference, though."

"I don't care for blackmail, Davis." Morton's voice had a hostile ring and Davis wondered if it was the Sioux that caused it, or himself telling of them.

"Call it what you want," he said. "Take it up with Ellis or Sisson; I'm just the messenger."

"I will, goddamn it," Morton said. "We can't stop to coddle every damned savage from here to the Columbia."

"It pays sometimes," Davis said, and then thought, what the hell. He stood in his stirrups, looking for the pair of thoroughbreds. "Ellis thinks you might dirty your horses some," he said when he picked them up. "The Sioux got a lame one, an' might be lookin' for a trade."

"What?" Morton gave a short, sharp laugh. "Ruin their coats? He's out of his head."

"Best they don't see what you got; they might get a hanker for 'em."

"You just tell Ellis I'll put them inside the circle, and put their blankets on."

"Thaddeus, perhaps . . ." Molly Morton started in to say, but didn't finish it because her husband cut her short with a wave of his hand.

"If you don't mind, Molly," he said without looking at her.

"Maybe you better tell Ellis what you got in mind," Davis said.

"I'll be responsible; they're mine, you know."

"Uh huh. One gone, two to go, Shouldn't take long."

Davis rode off before the thing went any farther. He'd done what Ellis had sent him for, and he was on the verge of getting himself mixed up in it. Was it his job to wheedle Morton into doing what was sensible? How come them as had the most success in their old land got so stupid in a new one?

Then he turned the mare and looked at the wagons in the circle, waiting for the Sioux, at the kids and women looking out, and the men standing with their rifles, showing brave, but somehow anxious, too. And swore.

Morton had run his horses into the middle now, the scarlet blankets more gaudy than the Sioux, themselves, in war paint. Of a sudden it came to him that Morton was putting the train in danger, that he had no right to do that. That being the man he was, he likely knew that for himself, but didn't give a damn. Whatever secret hates and loathings he had inside him were going to get them all in trouble.

The notion came at the same time, and he waved to catch Emmet's eye, then turned back toward the wagons. By the time he got around to the river side of the corral, he saw Morton joining Ellis and the council, far out, a hundred yards away. When Emmet got there he already had a wagon tongue down, the blankets off, and was leading the animals through the gap.

"Say, this ought to be good," Emmet said, and Davis knew the other man had caught onto it.

"I planned it to be," he said. "Get that bucket over there."

"Goin' to be an angry man time the moon comes over the Platte tonight," Emmet said when he came back with the wooden bucket in his hand.

"We'll ford that creek when we come to it."

"Damned if he shouldn't be grateful for the time we take."

"You'd think so, wouldn't you? Bet he ain't, though."

"Only a mean sonofabitch would think otherwise."

"I got a feelin' that describes our man."

They came to the river and Emmet held the hackamores while Davis waded in. He threw a bucket or two of water on each of the horses before Emmet led them back to a patch of dusty ground. A cloud went into the air as the two of them dug into it with their hands.

"They don't seem to mind it none," Emmet said between throws.

"Just like ordinary animals, at that."

"You'd figure they'd look down their noses at this treatment."

"Common as buffalo chips beneath the skin."

"Speakin' of chips, we ought to have a few."

"Hell, take a look."

"I mean fresh ones; them nice soft ones go good with horse hair."

"I guess that does it." Davis straightened up for the last time, and looked at the coating of dust sticking to the wet hides.

"Filthy things," Emmet said. "Bet they ain't felt better since they started out."

"Keep the flies off, anyway."

Davis gathered up the hackamores and Emmet took the bucket and they headed back. When they came to the herd being held outside the circle, Davis turned the horses loose and pointed them out to one of the herders standing guard. Then they put the wagon tongue in place, and mounted up.

"Have a look," Emmet said when they'd gone fifty yards or so. "She's seen us; she's smilin' at us." Emmet swept his hat off and bowed from the waist.

Davis turned his head and saw Molly Morton looking at them from the wagon seat. He was in a good mood now, and he thought to play a rise out of Emmet, telling him how things could be with her.

"You know . . ." he started in to say, then changed his mind in the middle of it, thinking it was too much like an old man looking back and counting coup on every roll in the hay he'd ever had.

Emmet was looking at him now, waiting for him to get along with it.

"Nice teeth," Davis said, and touched the flanks of the mare with his heels as he heard the far shout.

"Look wise, boys!" the shout came past the wagons. "Here they come!"

THIRTEEN

Andy kept the council members at the gathering point while Ellis stood out farther in the clear, another fifty yards. He held his ceremonial pipe in his hand, the stone calumet, and Davis saw him ramming tobacco into it and pounding it so the approaching Sioux could see he was a peaceful man, and one who wished to smoke with them. When the pilot nodded, Davis and Emmet rode out to join him.

"I guess they're about ready," Davis said. "Andy's got 'em all now."

"I seen 'em. Thanks for makin' the rounds."

Davis looked at the Sioux, a hundred yards away, coming at a walk, still mounted on the horses. As a sign they understood the meaning of Ellis's pipe, they had their bows pushed into their quivers, and their lances up. One of them held what looked to be an old French fusil across his legs, and the first lance had a new scalp swinging from it. None of them had saddles, but only woven thongs around the horses' middles, which they could grab, and hackamores instead of bridles.

"About even up," Davis said, marking seven braves again, and adding up the total of the council, himself and the other two now waiting.

"It's about right," Ellis said. He held the stone pipe high, being exaggerated in his motions so the Sioux could see them clearly. "We don't want to crowd 'em none. Did Morton fix them horses?"

"We figured we could do it better," Emmet said.

"How's that?" Ellis turned to look at him, his face blank with the question.

"He didn't think so much of it," Davis said. "So we waited 'til he shoved off, then fixed 'em our own selves."

"Is that right? Good for you." Ellis's mustache horns lifted upward with his grin.

"He was goin' to leave 'em in the circle with their blankets on."

"Goddamn fool," Ellis said. "I don't get that man at all."

"Ain't many do, I guess," Davis said. "He's goin' to kick on it though."

"Let him," Ellis said. "So long's they're dusted for the smoke; be dark time we're through with it."

Davis looked around again; the council members were coming forward, keeping pace with the nearing Sioux.

"Andy do the talkin'?"

"Through me," Ellis said. "I'll interpret. Do you

savvy Sioux talk?"

"Some, I can get the thought of it. Can't make it, though."

"Well, it don't make any difference. I'll make it clear as I can. Better get down, I guess."

Now the Sioux were close, stepping down and giving their horses over to the bent-up brave to hold while the others talked. Davis saw the dark skins, the feathers in their hair and the paint, red and black, streaked on their bodies. They wore clouts and moccasins and their faces said nothing underneath the smears and streaks of paint. When the council came up, there was a moment of waiting, of sizing up, like a pair of strange dogs smelling around each other, curious, but wary, too.

The Sioux were young, Davis saw again, as one of them exchanged the sign of peace with Ellis, and as the rest of them got arranged in a circle on the ground. Young and full of ginger, and he thought again how they could be more sure of this thing if only they had an old chief along with them.

Ellis lit the pipe and made the sign in the four directions before he took a suck and passed it to the first brave. The smoke curled up from the bowl and the coal glowed as he drew inward, and the smoke eased out of his mouth around the stem. From brave to brave, around the circle, back to the whites again. The heat came through the stone, and the spit ran along the stem.

Davis watched the wagon men take their turns at it. When you smoked the calumet you had to think about some other thing the farther off the better. You had to put your mind away from dwelling on the saliva running down, on the vermin in the mouths of them you smoked with; you couldn't wonder what the Indians might be giving with the spit.

Most of them did pretty good. The jaws tightened up, the lips pursed some; Drew looked like he was doing it for God and God alone, and Mabry closed his eyes. All of them wiped the stem good before they put it in their mouths. When it came to him, Davis took a pull and passed it on to Morton, who sat beside him. The Sioux were staring, blank and Asiatic.

"I'll be damned if I will," Morton said into the silence, and Davis felt the wagon men tighten up, like a spring had been compressed.

"Come on, now, we're pretty near finished." Ellis spoke without looking at him, quietly.

"I'm not going to fill myself with Indian spit," Morton said. "By God, they might even have the pox."

"They might have a lot of things," Andy said. "We take our chances."

"We can't have these children sore at us," Ellis said. "Smoke up, now, hear?"

"To hell with them. I'm not afraid."

"I ain't either," Ellis said. "Not this handful, but there's a heap more down with the buffalo."

"I think you're overdoing it, Ellis. They're only oriental nomads."

"Maybe so, but they can keep you from gettin' on to Oregon, if they take the notion."

Ellis's voice had a grained edge, and maybe that got to Morton, that or the pointlessness of the argument. Either way, Morton wrapped his fist around the mouthpiece and put his lips to the curl of his hand. He took a shallow pull, then spat the smoke out in a fat puff.

"There, goddamn it, take your pipe."

"Like to see you smoke with a Digger," Ellis said.

With the greeting part of it over, Ellis began talking to the Sioux. He told the braves he spoke for Sisson, whom he indicated with his hand, and that the captain of the train was happy to meet his red brothers in the council circle. He was glad they had come to smoke the calumet with him, and they were welcome to spend the night along the river, if they wished to. He explained that the wagons were on their way to the far salt sea, and were making their way through the land belonging to the Sioux in peace. They did not seek trouble; yet if trouble came they had plenty of men and rifles to take care of it. Ellis spoke in his chest and belly, and made slow, embracing motions with his hands and arms.

A short, barrel-chested brave with a scarred face spoke for the Sioux.

They, too, were full of gladness, so he said. It was pleasing indeed to meet with the white men in this manner, to smoke and talk. The buffalo had kept them very busy this year and they did not often have the chance to strike the white man's trail beside the river.

Yes, their hearts were happy, he explained again when Ellis had put the first words into white talk, but in them lay a measure of sadness, too, for the hated Pawnees had been encountered farther south, and in the skirmish one of their number had been carried to the spirit land; moreover, the departed brother's horse had been injured, too.

When Ellis translated this Davis heard Morton's short, hard laugh again.

"Simple poetic justice. If they hadn't been running the buffalo they never would have met the Pawnees. Ask him why they were doing that."

"Not much point in it," Ellis said. "We'd best play dumb about the buffalo."

"They've got gall, begging sympathy," Morton said. "They've got what they deserved."

"All right, Morton, lay off." It was Andy speaking, looking big and angry, squatting on the ground.

"Don't upset yourself, Sisson," Morton said, making light of it. "It was just an observation."

Ellis talked again. Davis heard his voice descend, saw his hands and arms move, heard the sound come out in gutturals and rumbles. Ellis was expressing sorrow for the dead brother, for the injured horse. He knew there would be mourning in the lodges, and he hoped the white brothers might give a few things to the aggrieved ones to show their feelings. When Ellis motioned, Sisson passed the articles from the canvas sack—a bag of colored beads, some cheap knives, a handful of copper bells, vermilion, and a hand axe.

The speaking brave accepted these and divided them among the others. When he spoke to Ellis again he asked for whisky.

"Whisky?" It was Morton again, surprised and showing it.

"It's all right. It's watered." Sisson held the small keg up, and pulled the cork out.

"I thought ours was strictly medicinal," Morton argued.

"This is medicine, of a sort," Ellis said. He held the tin cup while Sisson filled it, then gave it to the speaking brave, who drank noisily, and passed it on.

"By God, Ellis, I don't approve of this." Morton was all of a flurry now, like a turkey with its fan spread.

"I don't either, exactly," Ellis said, not looking at him, but at the braves, "but I aim to please."

"It's an arbitrary move," Morton said with feeling. "You've gone over our heads. The council should have decided this."

"There wasn't any time." Andy Sisson spoke quietly while he filled the cup again, and held the keg tail-end up to show that it was empty. Then he set it down and blazed at Morton. "For Christ's sake, shut up. We can't plan everything. Sometimes we got to take things as they come."

From the sudden flustered look of him, it seemed as if Morton would have more to say, but it was the Sioux themselves who shut him up. The speaking brave was now making wide movements of his arm, and it got to the wagon men that he was talking of their horses. Through Ellis, he said their injured horse would make a poor showing if they returned to camp with it; they would like to make a trade, since the white brother's heart was good.

"Well, how about it?" Ellis said when it was clear that everybody understood. "Anyone got an old nag he don't want?"

"I'll speak out on that, too," Morton said, as if he dared anyone to stop him. "They don't get anything I brought with me."

"Kind of a big order, at that, don't you think, Andy?" Gideon Drew had doubt in his voice, his hand rubbing on his chin.

"Could be," Andy said. "In time it might mean a lot to the man that gave it up."

"Mountains comin', an' all," Mabry said, "it's hard to know what might be needed, and what might be spared."

Because no one went beyond that, it looked as if all had said their piece, but Sisson waited a moment to see if anything would be added.

"I guess we better let them have the mule, then," he said to Ellis. "That horse they got ain't much, but it can't be a hell of a lot worse than what they're gettin'."

"It don't make no difference," Ellis said, "They'll eat the mule, anyway; everyone'll be ahead on the trade."

Ellis put the trade talk into Siouian, and from what he got of it, Davis learned that Andy's black mule was the finest animal that ever fed on Missouri grass. Its strength was such that it could pull a loaded prairie schooner at a full gallop by its own self, and with a rider up, could about outrun any horse they'd brought along. Furthermore, it was very young, and its firm flesh would be mighty tasty.

When they'd talk it over among themselves, the Sioux braves nodded their heads to show that they accepted. Maybe they thought to get a horse out of it, but a mule feast was a tempting thing. The talking brave made the point clear to Ellis, and then made the sign for the council's end. The braves got up and began to put their trinkets into bags and pouches, or to wrap them in the blankets they'd left on their horses.

"It didn't go so bad, did it?" Andy Sisson said, looking around to see how it sat with everyone; relieved and smiling now.

"I'd say you come out well ahead," Davis said. "You might make something of that little paint pony, if his leg turns out all right."

"I was worried we might wind up eatin' that thing our own selves," Ellis said. "Hardly good for anything else."

Dark was coming on and some of the men were moving toward the wagons, toward the evening fires; but Morton lingered, himself appearing pleased at the turn the thing had taken.

"I'm glad I used my head," he said to Ellis, his tone giving out he'd put one over on the pilot and was pleased to let him know about it. "I'd be half the night cleaning up my horses otherwise."

Ellis was watching the Indians heading toward the river to make their camp, and he didn't turn around. At first it looked like Morton had got his dander up, because the muscles of his jaw bulged out, like he was clamping down. Then Davis saw the glint in the pilot's eye, and knew he was trying to keep from laughing.

Shenandoah, I love your daughter,
Away, the rolling river,
Shenandoah, I love your daughter,
And away, I'm bound away
Across the wide Missouri.

A pair of fiddles was working out the tune, and the stars shone clear and hard against the prairie sky. Mostly the people had finished their evening meal, and the young ones were being bedded down in the wagons or in the tents which some had pitched inside the circle. The men were hunkered down in little groups about the fires, talking of the day's ride, of the smoke with the Sioux. Over all Davis heard the music and a few singing voices tying them together. Davis couldn't see any dancing. The people probably thought they would be too showy before the Sioux, camped down the river, a quarter mile away, eating the mule.

And away, I'm bound away,
Across the wide Missouri.

He rolled the antelope haunch, which he shared with Ellis and Emmet, into the tarp, and pushed it under the bed of Sisson's wagon with the other gear, against the time they'd load it on the pack horse in the morning. Then he took the coffee pot, sloshed it through a pan of water, and shook it in the air to get the worst of the wetness off. When he finished, he dropped it with the pan in a tow sack, and slung it under the wagon bed atop the antelope.

"Not a bad feed," he said to Emmet. "I always say, you're as good as ary a woman."

"You don't dast not like it, so long as I'm doin' the fixin'," Emmet said. He was cleaning out the Dutch oven, cutting the cooking grease with sand.

"Some truth to that. But I mean it, Emmet. I don't see why you ain't married up to some man, doin' for him."

"Maybe I don't shine in other ways."

"Most men think of their bellies, anyway. You could work out somethin'."

"Come to think of it, you're right, Aaron. Hell, yes, I'd get by."

Davis put tobacco in his pipe, and looked around as he tamped it with his thumb. Away in the dark, between two wagons, a shadow moved. He kept looking at the outline of the guard and the rifle held at the ready while he reached over and pulled a burning stick from the fire, and lit the pipe.

"What time you on, Emmet?" he said then.

"Midnight, damn it all. Nothin' like a good night's sleep split down the middle." Emmet got up from the ground and took the Dutch oven over to the tow sack beneath the wagon. When he had it stowed, he pulled his blanket out and spread it on the ground. "You got it now, ain't you?"

"Uh huh. A few minutes yet. That's 'cause us old bastards need our sleep."

Emmet was rolled in the blanket, his hat folded underneath his head. Already his eyes were closed, his face smoothing out with the sleep coming over him, and Davis tried to think back to the time when he had been like that; when he could take things as they came, no matter what, then put them out of his mind when sleep was wanted.

There was still time, and he thought to check with Ellis before he went on guard. The pilot was sitting with Andy Sisson at another fire halfway between the wagon and the tent that Andy'd pitched. Esther and the Piper boy had turned in, it looked like, and just the two of them were squatting there when Davis wandered over.

"Coffee, Aaron?" Andy said, and half-reached for the pot bubbling in the flames.

"No, thanks. Keep your seat. I'm goin' on guard in a minute."

"You heard from Morton yet, about them horses?" Ellis took his pipe from his mouth, and smoke came out with the words.

"No, damn it, an' I been wonderin'. Don't know as I should ask or not."

"I thought sure the camp'd be in an uproar by now," Andy said. "Hard to figger how he'd keep quiet after findin' out."

"I wouldn't jump him out on it," Ellis said. "Sleepin' dogs are better left alone. Likely, he'll speak his piece when he's ready to."

"We can count on it," Davis said. He looked around, wondering if the dark contained a clue, but he couldn't find the Morton wagon in the circle.

"Jim was sayin' we ain't too far from Laramie," Andy said to him when he turned around again. "Four, five days with decent goin'."

"Figger on five, with the pass around Scott's Bluff," Ellis said. "Even so, we're gettin' there."

“Yeah, we are,” Andy said, but the way he said it made Davis think the distance still weighed heavy on him, as though a lot could happen between here and Laramie. “I’ll be glad when we shake these Sioux.”

“They’ll be gone ’fore daylight,” Ellis said. “Shouldn’t be much to worry over now.”

“I guess there ain’t, at that,” Andy said. “We got plenty guards out. An’ the stock is all hobbled.”

Davis walked away with the thought of Morton’s horses sticking in his head. He was thinking now he ought to find out what was holding Morton back from raising hell; but on the other hand, he didn’t want to get his neck stuck out by asking him.

There was a fire here and there, with people gathered still, though a lot of them were folding up. Up at four, roll and rock all day, and a body could hardly stay awake through supper, even though they’d toughened up considerable to what they were a month and more ago. Them as sat around the fires still, listening to the music were keeping quiet for the most part, staring at the flames as though they could see the trail awinding through them, going hack to Minnesota, or Indiana, or wherever it might lead to. Maybe wondering if they’d done the right thing in setting out. A fire put thoughts in a man’s mind, you couldn’t get around it.

Then he came into the shadow of a wagon, and saw the woman standing at the other end of it. He couldn’t make her features out, but the figure told him it was

Molly Morton; that and the way she turned away, as though she'd recognized him and was making off. He caught up with her and reached out to take her arm.

"Please," she said, as she stopped again. "We can't do this. It's not right."

"Do what? I'm not doing anything." He could see her face now, because she was looking up at him, but he couldn't tell exactly what he found there.

"You know what I mean." She said it in a low voice.

"You didn't seem to mind before. I thought you liked it."

"It's wrong, no matter what I thought." She stood away from him, her hands clasped in front of her, as though she didn't trust him, or herself, perhaps.

"As a matter of fact, I was thinkin' of your husband," Davis said, thinking now that he could play it, too, since she had started it.

"Oh?" Molly Morton said, and he wondered what he heard—whether she was put out that he hadn't come to see her, after all, or relieved to know it. Often as not, a woman meant just the opposite of what she said.

"You saw me an' Emmet fix your husband's horses. I wondered why we hadn't heard him yellin'."

"He's with them now," Molly Morton said. "He was angry enough, all right."

"Where?" Davis looked around, half expecting Morton to appear with them, grandly walking in their blankets.

"Over there." She began to walk, keeping well away from Davis as he followed her. When they came to the end of the wagon she stopped him in the gap between that one and the one behind it. He looked across the tongue, through the hobbled livestock toward the river lying dull and smooth in the first light of the moon still to rise.

"On the bank. Can you see him?"

"Good God!" He saw them now, the horses standing at the edge, and Morton with them, trying to get the dirt off. They were more than fifty yards away, but he could see them.

Then he turned around and looked at her. "I don't get it. This ain't the Thaddeus Morton I know."

"I told him I did it."

"You?" He said it slow, he was surprised, and then he felt the smile come on his face, and knew she saw it.

"Don't be so conceited. There's more than a hundred people in this train. Any trouble Thaddeus might start would be hard on everyone. There was nothing personal in it."

"Sure, sure," Davis said. He felt the smile spread, and saw the look come in her face as she imagined what it meant. He caught the movement of her breasts against the darkness underneath, as anger made her breathing deep and fast.

When he took her shoulder she tried to pull away, but Davis held her. Then he bent his head down and found her lips and kissed her hard. He felt her lips crushed and bruised beneath his own, and felt the moistness, too, as the fragrance of her filled him. She was fighting him, and once she broke away, the "No," weak and breathy, but he found her lips again and the resistance ended, and he felt the heat in him rise high and choking as she pushed against him, alive and strong. He felt her arms grow tight around his neck and her fingers moving in his hair.

"I hate you." She whispered it against his lips.

"Don't talk." He pushed his lips down, trying to silence her.

"Devil, devil."

"Shut up."

Then she stopped, and kissed him back again, her mouth weak, then strong and hungry; her arms came tighter around his neck. When he felt her tears against his check he was astonished, but he knew he could have anything he wanted.

FOURTEEN

Ellis had a time of it with sleep. For a long while it was pitch and turn for him, on one side first and then the other. Sometimes he'd be lying on his back, his hands clasped beneath his head, watching how the stars burned brighter as the fires in the circle died out one by one. Then he'd try his side again, and eye the wagons hulking dim and shapeless in the dark—until the moon rose in the east and made them come alive with the changing light and shadow creeping over them. The Sioux camp was beyond what he could see, but when he closed his eyes he could see them in his mind again; see them coming on their horses, sitting at the smoke, and see the fresh scalp fluttering at the lancehead. Maybe it was the trophy that was holding him awake tonight, the sight of it, and the thought of what it meant; it was like a landmark of a sort, in a way as full of meaning as the Chimney and the other monuments of the trail, a reminder of many an old remembrance, the passing of another.

Off and on he'd doze, but would awake again. He was halfway in between, but came suddenly alert when Davis came off guard. His moccasins moved silently across the circle, the look of him half-real, half-shadow by the moonlight. Ellis saw him nudge Emmet with his foot, and when the younger man came out of sleep like a cat flipping over and landing upright, the memory came, part amusement, part longing, of a time when he had been that way.

Goddamn, he was getting old, to judge by the thoughts that was crowding him tonight.

"Time sure come in a hurry," he heard Emmet say.

"An' slow from now on," Davis said, half-laughing.

"Ain't that the truth, though? That's somethin' for a

smart man to figure out."

Emmet was up now, sliding into his leather shirt, getting his rifle and powder horn together. Alongside of him, Davis had got his blanket from beneath the wagon, and was rolling in it.

"They finish with the mule?" Emmet said when he was set to go. "The Sioux, I mean?"

"I expect they have, can't say for sure. I was on the other side, an' couldn't see 'em." Davis had risen to his elbow, and now he stayed there as if he'd just remembered something, and had more to say. "Hey, Emmet, Morton's wife told him she done the fixin' on the horses."

"His wife?" Emmet stood there looking down at Davis, and Ellis could see the outline of his face, expressing wonder. "I'll be damned."

"That's why we didn't hear from him."

"I guess it is." Emmet hefted his rifle. "Where'd you learn that?"

"She told me. I run into her on my way to guard."

"Oh?" There was a pause, like Emmet might be speculating on that. "How come?" he added.

"How come what?" Davis said.

"How come she done it?"

"For the good of the outfit, is what she said." Davis let his elbow out from under him and Ellis heard the easy humor in him. "For the good of the outfit, Emmet boy. G'night."

Emmet became a shape in the dark, a shadow. When he was one with the shadows and gone, Ellis hunched over on his side. "Aaron?" He said it quietly, near a whisper. But a few feet lay between them.

The shape of Davis moved and rolled, and Ellis saw his face. "Hell, Jim, you awake? I bet I done it comin' in."

"It's been off an' on ever since I turned in."

"Must be moonstruck," Davis said.

"At my age, too. Still full of foolishness."

"You hear what I told Emmet? About Morton's wife?"

"Yeah, I heard. Sounds like some woman."

"She is," Davis said, and there was that easy humor once again.

Ellis thought before he spoke. Hell, it wasn't his business, but night was a strange time, and a man could say things then he wouldn't think of during daylight.

"Aaron?"

"Huh."

"Have a care, son," Ellis said, and halfway wished he hadn't.

It was a piece of time before Davis said anything again, and Ellis wondered if he'd made an enemy. Sometimes good intentions could lead a body to a mess of trouble.

"Yeah," Davis said after the pause. It was low and drawn out, is though each part of the sound had been planned. "You're right, goddamn it."

"Not my affair, Aaron, you know that. But if I see, so can others."

"I know. You're right. I thought plenty on it. Damn, a man gets mixed up, don't he, though?"

"Ain't no help at all, sometimes," Ellis said, and was pleased to turn the edge of criticism by the saying of it.

"Seems so, don't it?" Davis said. "I'll work it out, though, somehow."

It was a place to let it die, a time to try for sleep again, but there was the other thing, still, and he thought Davis ought to know. He hadn't thought to speak to anyone about it; it had to do with him, a part of him, in its peculiar way. But he felt kindlier toward Davis now, closer somehow, like he knew him better, and he felt he ought to know.

"Still awake, Aaron?"

"Yeah, Jim, I'm here."

"Remember when I took the mule over?"

"To the Sioux camp?"

"Uh huh. After the smoke. I seen that scalp again, an' asked about it."

"On the lancehead. I remember. What about it?"

"It belonged to Antelope."

"Antelope? The old Pawnee? Christ, Jim, I'm sure sorry."

"It's all right," Ellis said. He was on his back again, his head cradled in his clasped hands, looking up. Damned if he wasn't drowsy of a sudden. Must be he had to spill that bit 'fore sleep would come. "It's the way she goes, is all. It's the way she goes."

Then he slept, so deep it seemed he scarcely closed his eyes before he woke again. But now the moon was gone and there were early-morning stirrings in the circle. The sky was shot with stars more glittering than in the middle of the night, and the black of it was like a cave that had no end, except along the east where gray was fuzzing up.

He rolled out and pulled his moccasins on to make the early rounds. He shapes of others were moving here and there slow and careful in the dark. Near the tailgate of a wagon a man stood with his legs apart, facing east, and Ellis wondered if the sight of dawn approaching gave him inspiration for what he did there. Inside a tent, a child cried out, fussing at the thought of being pulled from sleep. In front of it, a woman raked up the ashes of a dead fire, about to kindle another one for breakfast. He glimpsed the long-bodied older Drew boy turning his old man's oxen out to graze, and it occurred to him the Indians must be gone.

At the edge of camp he met Emmet coming off guard.

"They're gone, all right," the young man said in answer to Ellis's question. "Half an hour or so, it was. I seen 'em goin' off across the valley."

"For the bluffs?" Ellis asked him. The gray light was pushing up more now, and spreading out, with a touch of color at the deep horizon. It would be another clear day, the thought came, clear and hot.

"Pretty near as they come in," Emmet said. "Couldn't see 'em too well—they was all bunched-up like in the dark—but they was goin' south for sure."

"Likely seen the last of 'em, then." They were heading back to breakfast now, and with the Sioux gone Ellis picked up the thought of other things, of the wagons catching up and lining out, of the trail winding on ahead, of a proper nooning place, of camp again when evening came. In just the time he'd taken to look around, the deep dark had turned gray all over, and nearly everyone was up. He smelled bacon cooking somewhere, which made his stomach growl. He heard a coffee pot fall and clang, and then a sleep-thick voice cuss because of it. The livestock, hobbles off, were moving out to graze.

Davis had the cooking gear set up, the fire going. The coffee pot was bubbling, and there came a simmer from within the Dutch oven sitting on the deep coals raked up from the night before.

"The least I could do," Davis said when the other two came up. "A man comin' off guard don't deserve to get stuck right away."

"Hell, you just couldn't wait, is all," Ellis said, squatting down to let the fire warmth soak into him, to get the thick, hot coffee smell in his nose. "But I'm glad you done it."

"I always had you marked as a big-belly man," Emmet said to Davis. "You got anything original goin' in that pot?"

"Just warmed-over biscuits, but you made 'em, so don't kick to me. That bacon, though, that was my thought."

"This high plains air really goes to the man's head, now, don't it?" Ellis said.

"Every man shows it in a different way," Emmet said. "It took a nice twist with Aaron, though, given what he fixed is edible."

They were squatting down around the fire, starting in. Davis took the bacon out, and then the biscuits, and the smell of breakfast in the early morning air became a sudden richness mingling with the steaming coffee pouring out. Ellis held the hot can gingerly in his one hand and ate the bacon and the biscuits with the other, settling back upon his haunches and thinking now that this particular moment in the early dawn was the best part of the new day coming on. When everything was fresh and new again, the country soft and promising to look upon, the colors gentle in their shading, deep where the shadows fell. When the call of a single, lonely bird became the only sound on earth, and the sight of an antelope coming in to drink the most beautiful thing a man could hope to see.

Ellis turned his head, the can poised, when the sound came, far off.

"What was that?"

The other two were listening, too, sitting like life had left them of a sudden, and it came again.

"Someone shoutin', it sounds like," Davis said.

"Trouble somewhere." Ellis heard it clear that time, a shout, sure, and then another; he was on his feet and looking toward the source of it, over east.

Then he saw the movement coming toward the circle from beyond the wagons, the men, Morton out in front, with the others coming after.

"A horse stole!" The shout came ahead of the moving men, and Ellis heard, already knowing whose it was. "The Sioux got one of Morton's thoroughbreds!"

Ellis spoke to be heard above the rumble of the wagons, moving out. It was clear day now, with the sun well up, and the sign was plain. He took his time, wanting to be right, and no matter that Morton fumed and fretted next to him. Davis and Emmet lingered with their horses a little to the side, the look of them saying they didn't want to get involved, but that they wouldn't shy off either should something develop out of this. Off a ways, between them and the train, Andy sat his horse undecided-like, as if he knew he should be riding along the line, yet felt he ought to be here, too. Finally he jerked his head a time or two, like it made his mind up for him, and cantered over.

"Moccasins been here," Ellis said again, and pointed out the imprints where the Indian had come along the river bank. "Pigeon-toed and flat-footed. Goin' for a look-see at the night herd."

"I had my horses at the river last night," Morton said. "I had to get that dirt off. That savage must have seen me."

"Could have been that way," Ellis said. "He was over here for somethin'."

"Don't see how he could miss you," Andy said, the tone giving out he thought this a poor time to dawdle along behind the wagons, with the day begun and the Sioux maybe still in the country. "You should have left it on. Likely, you'd still have him now."

"They aren't oxen, Sisson. They weren't born to wallow."

"Be a lot less trouble if they were," Andy said right back at him. "For all of us."

Ellis left them wrangling with one another, following after the tracks. When he saw the first set returning to the dead Sioux camp he swung away from the river, watching out for more, farther in. He made a circle of the bedding ground and covered the whole of the morning grazing area before he found what he was looking for. He was now inland a couple of hundred yards, southeast, and the others were trailing after, but keeping back.

"Been here, too," he said when the rest of them came up. "There's more out further, where he likely waited before he made his grab."

"Figure he lay low out here 'til they was turned out?" Andy asked.

"Must have," Ellis said. "Made his pick last night at the river, an' then cut back from the rest of his bunch when they was headin' out this mornin'."

"Pretty smart," Andy said. "An' guts aplenty."

"They're well-known on both counts." Ellis put his hands on his hips and looked far away at the bluffs rising up, and wondered how far off the Sioux would be.

"When'd you turn your horses out?" he said to Morton, when he looked away again.

"When I understood the Indians were gone," Morton said, right away implying that any bad judgment had not been his. "I kept them in the circle last night, and turned them out when the others did."

"They was gone half an hour afore the first stock went out." Emmet and Davis had come in closer, and Emmet spoke for the first time, saying it as though he took Morton's remarks as being personal.

"Mine was second out, after Drew's," Andy said. "And that was a good while after. How soon was yours out, anyway?"

"I didn't mark it by my watch, Sisson, after all,"

Morton said. "There were fifteen, twenty head out there; what difference does it make? I understood it was perfectly safe, and clearly it was not."

"Safe for any stock, save yours, it looks like," Ellis said. "That one come back to look for your stuff special."

"All right, now we know," Morton said, as if that much of it was beside the point. "What next?"

"Next we best catch up with the wagons," Andy said, and looking at him Ellis knew that Andy was fidgeting again, yearning toward the column moving onward in its dust; likely thinking he ought to be watching for the nooning place, watching out for grass and water. "Too bad," Andy added as an afterthought.

"Too bad, you say?" and Morton's voice was thick and swollen now, like he had a bone caught in his throat. "Well, that's not good enough. I want that horse back."

"That's askin' somethin'," Andy said. He was sitting straighter now, giving Morton the whole of his attention, and it came to Ellis that Morton was going to make a point of this. It came to him that Morton had been waiting to push himself at them again, and this was it.

"They'd be a good ways off by now," Ellis said. He spoke it easy, feeling his way, aware again of his lack of experience with men like Morton. He wished he could tell which way he was going to jump.

"I don't give a damn if they're in China," Morton said. "I want that horse."

"Hell, man, you heard Ellis," Andy said.

"They sure ain't goin' to hang around none," Emmet said.

Then it seemed Morton came unhinged, as if he didn't give a damn for anything just then, but the rage that was burning holes in him. Maybe it was Emmet speaking up that touched him off, half-shouting in a high, loose voice.

"I said I didn't give a damn and that's what I mean! You men lost that horse for me and you men are going to get it back!"

"Hold on, there, Morton," Andy said, loud and getting angry, too.

"Hold on, be damned, Sisson! These two"—and Morton's arm flailed toward the hunters—"got them dirtied up. I got it from a herder who saw them do it."

"Christ, I wish they'd stuck them in a sinkhole in the Platte," Andy said, but Morton went right on as if he didn't hear a bit of it.

"If those two had left them alone, they would have been safe inside the circle!"

"I doubt that," Ellis said, and now he knew he was in it, too. "I thought the word went out your wife done that dustin' job."

"A lie, told to prevent friction, so she said." Then Morton turned his dark face on Davis. "A queer reason, don't you think?"

Davis ran his reins through his hands and didn't speak out right away. His eyes seemed to take in Morton and the river and Ellis wondered if he saw himself throwing dust on the horses once again, or maybe Morton's wife held tight against him.

"We done it, all right," he said in a moment, and he said it quiet as though it didn't matter what Morton thought. "If you'd let 'em be, you'd still have that horse now; but, like you say, we done it." When Davis gathered in the reins and mounted up he looked down again. "Just to stop this goddamned screamin' I'll take a look up there beyond the hills. I don't promise nothin', but I'll take a look."

"Wait a minute," Ellis heard himself say. "I had the notion. You done it on my say-so. I'll go."

"I'm against it either way," Andy said positively. "Might something happen."

"Small chance of that," Ellis said. "They ain't in no tarrying mood, I doubt they can be found."

"Then, why go at all?" Andy wanted to know.

" 'Cause there's always the chance," Davis said. "I'm goin', Jim," he said to Ellis. "Me an' Emmet really done it."

"No, y'ain't. If anyone's goin' up, it's me. You don't know Sioux talk, remember?"

"So?" Davis said. "I make sense of it."

"But you can't talk back."

"How come you need Sioux talk when you just said they won't be found?" Andy said.

" 'Cause the chance is always there, like Aaron said."

"Hey, hold on!" It was Andy calling out as Ellis swung on up and necked his horse around.

"Take it easy, Andy," Ellis said, looking down at him, amused now at the look of real alarm on the captain's face. "I need fresh air anyway. I'll see you at the nooning; Aaron'll spell me out 'til I get back."

"Hell, Jim, I don't like it this way," Davis said. "So what if I can't speak the tongue. I can make sign talk, can't I?"

"Sure, but if you need talk at all what you got won't fill the bill."

"Watch it, then, Jim."

"Christ, I'm just goin' up to shoot a buffalo."

"I don't like this one bit, Jim," Andy said, still of a mood to call the whole thing off. "Y'ought to tell Morton to go straight to hell."

"He'll likely make it on his own," Ellis said, and for once the square, dark man held his tongue; he only stood there looking up at him as if it had all developed beyond what he'd expected.

He swung away, then, his hand held up as the horse began to move. Far off he saw the dust where the wagons lumbered on, where the cattle trudged, and he was all at once glad to be away from all that for a while.

Do him good to be alone on the plains for a time; he had so many queer, old-like thoughts these days he ought to air his head out good. He might even shoot a buffalo, at that, if he could find one. It was going to be a clear day, sure, like he'd figured, clear and hot. He rode away across the valley hoping there would be a breeze moving up along the bluffs.

FIFTEEN

Davis felt the morning swell with heat as the sun reached out of dawn and climbed; and he wondered why he should notice it so much today, and then thought it must be related to the stretch of time involved since Ellis had gone across the valley toward the bluffs. Time was seven different kinds of snails when there was something you were looking forward to, and today the heat became a measure of it.

Since Andy's head was turning on a swivel, forever facing south, he knew the captain had it, too, the feel of the sun saying it was late, causing his anxiety to grow like a plant coming up in spring and stretching out. Andy's being so obvious irritated him, pointing up his own concern, and he wished he'd concentrate on the way the trail wound out instead; yet Andy wouldn't be himself unless he took every little thing to heart and worried over it until it shaped up the way it was intended.

Now Andy was saying it again, for the third time in an hour, and hitching around to squint from his bluff face shaded by the wide hat. Davis saw the dark stain of sweat where the brim joined the crown, and Andy's eyes looking out half-closed against the glare of pallid earth and grass and the steep rim rising up where the plains began.

"Been gone a time, Aaron, seems to me."

"Pretty long ways up there." Davis made a point of facing forward, and sounding casual, as though the whole thing was just a notion Andy had.

"I know, but we could see him on the rimrock now, I'd think."

"Dependin' on how far in he went. If they was travelin' fast he'd have to go a piece."

"You really think he chased 'em?" And there was Andy in alarm again, as though he'd held an illusion concerning Ellis's purpose, and had just had it shattered for him.

"Sure, he did. That's what he went up there for, ain't it?"

Davis heard himself speak rough, and immediately felt badly, but he couldn't help it. He thought now he might have been deceived his own self, and he could speak that way when he tried to cover up. It wasn't hard to fall in with Ellis's disarming way of doing things, his seeming unconcern with matters that might be difficult or have a flair of danger to them. Sometimes he seemed to wrap it around him like a layer of winter fat, so that nothing ever quite got at him.

All at once he knew he had this thing the same as Andy, and maybe more, because he was familiar with the high bluffs and the plains beyond, because he knew how long it ought to take the pilot to look around, and even talk a while should he find the Sioux. Hell, yes, Ellis should have showed; it was nearly noon.

He turned his horse around and stopped, staring out; Andy drew beside him and the two of them faced across the valley toward the palisades and broken rock which seemed to breathe in the heat waves shaking far away.

"I better go on up," he said. He wasn't pretending anything any more.

"All right; I guess you better. Christ." Andy looked around, as if a solution to this problem lay near at hand, if he could only get a grip on it. Then he faced the bluffs again, which had the answer, likely, but wouldn't give it.

"Any place around here looks, all right for nooning," Davis said, and he was aware of trying to concentrate on known, familiar things.

"Uh huh, good grass; we can dig a well if the kegs are low," Andy said, and Davis knew that Andy was being a party to it, too.

"Emmet can help out, should anything come up.

He's around somewhere."

"He was riding back a ways," Andy said; he rose in his stirrups looking east along the wagons as if Emmet's whereabouts were the most important thing on earth just then.

"I guess you might as well keep goin' 'til we show, or you get to night camp." Davis was being careful to make a "we" of it, and felt uneasy doing so.

"All right. We want to get as close to the pass as we can."

"That's right," Davis said, and he nudged the mare with his heels to start her moving. This going off was getting too elaborate.

"Take it easy." Andy had to shout because the mare was yards away and lifting into a canter.

Davis waved his arm once and turned around. He was going south and when he cleared the haze of dust he swung east and rode parallel to the wagons going past. He saw the kids and women leaning out, and the men walking with the oxen turn their heads, and he knew what was lying in their minds had sharpened up because of seeing him. The had been suspecting, he could tell, throughout the morning, likely, and now they knew.

He knew himself now, or feared, and he tried to push it back. There were a hundred things that Ellis could have gotten into, but there wasn't any point in going over them. The least of them—perhaps a shoe knocked off—only seemed to lead to something else, and should he lose himself in wondering he'd soon be dwelling on the ultimate disaster, and he wouldn't let himself consider that.

He was glad when the train was gone and he had the valley to himself. The mare was going at an easy canter, and he'd turned again, to intercept the trail of Ellis and the Indians before it struck the bluffs. He was aware of concentrating on the land so as to keep his thoughts in check, of sending his eye and mind out over the long reaches slanting up.

There was a slant here, he told himself, as though to make an argument about it. A long slant from the bluffs to the river bed, cut in lengthy shelves, so gradual he hardly noticed them; old beaches where the Platte had long ago meandered, grass-grown now but sand and gravel underneath. As though it was the first time he'd ever thought of it, he was struck with the air of age it all gave off—the benches cutting down since the beginning of forever, the few silvered limbs somehow escaped from the Indians' endless burning of the grass. And the islands in the river where the trees still stood, cottonwoods and willows, but gaunt and half-dead, many of them, looking wind-racked and burned out by the sun.

It was a place of beauty in its strange way, a place to remind a man how no account he was; and this remained with him when he came beneath the rim and saw the face of it all split and fractured, slowly graining into talus. He was moving slower now, scanning everything for sign, a part of him recalling the look of the country where the last night camp had been, and another aware of the antiquity embodied in the bluffs.

Then he recognized the camp ground against the river, far off, and saw the grass battered where the herd had grazed and the wagons turned. He was near now, and in a sandy place where only prickly pear could make a go of it, he found the first prints, shod and unshed, both. The tracks showed clear and plain, going through the lifting hills and toward the high bluffs rising vertical above.

Where the cliffs broke down there was a buffalo trail emerging from a defile with the horse prints overlaid clear upon the cloven ones. Because the defile was confining, he didn't have to watch the tracks and he let his eyes go up to the splintered rock, hot and tawny in the sun, and the bald, impoverished hills which opened on the plains. He couldn't divert his anxiety any more, and the hills and bluffs enclosing him intensified it, as though their bulk and silence suggested something sinister.

It was better when they opened up and he was rid of them. The plains rolled out beyond and he remembered now how he always seemed to be more comfortable in flat or rolling country, where the grass went out as far as he could see. High rocks brooding down, blocking out his vision, were like the deep forests in the east, where a man didn't have a view ahead, or around him even. It made him remember he felt easier in the open when there might be trouble in the offing.

After he trailed an hour he topped a rise, and far beyond another he saw the great birds wheeling black against the sky. He saw the birds and when he thought of what might be lying underneath the anxiety came to flood.

Without a clear thought, he pushed his feet against the mare, and sent her down. The long slope passed under in a swish of grass bending over and the hoofs pounding made a soft thudding in the wind rushing past his ears. Where the slope ran together with the shallow swale there lay a seam, and the mare jolted him in going over because his eyes were on the birds clear against the sky above the rise ahead. The birds held sharp to his eye until the next slope pitched up and the crest rose high to blot them out.

Then he topped the swell and the birds circled straight ahead, flying high. The mare swung along the new incline and Davis half-stood in his stirrups when he saw the dark mass lying in the grass beyond. He was not aware of the horse running any more, nor of his move to slow her down. He was looking at the richness in the earth where the blood had spilled, and the grass bent and flattened where the fight had raged. And the dark mass, Ellis, lying stripped of everything the Sioux could use.

Only half-believing, his mind's eye saw Ellis ripped apart and broken, yet still alive, too, and softly smiling as he hunkered by a fire in the evening. He saw him sitting at the smoke, looking half an Indian himself as his hands moved with the talk rumbling out of him, at the Big Blue far away in time when he held the mule tail black and glistening in the firelight. He wondered now if Ellis's scalp hung aside of Antelope's on the lance-head.

He gazed around, feeling slow and dull, and a hundred yards away he saw the pilot's horse sprawled out, the look of death plain even at that distance. Then he looked around again, more alert now that he accepted the fact of Ellis lying dead in the grass. Then he saw the movement, small but definite on the skyline.

When the Sioux party showed full he didn't feel surprised, even though he knew it was a planned maneuver, and knew that he was boxed. It all got across to him at once; yet he took it in now like he'd been warned of it. This bunch was capable of ambushing him. The thought came as he recalled their meanness because of what the Pawnees had done. Ambush would be a natural way to make a showing of themselves against a white, and he knew they'd do him in like they had Ellis if they could.

There were four and they were moving in to block

him from the river. The first two came from nearly northeast and the other pair down a rise lifting west, the lot of them moving fluidly across the brown grass, the high tips showing silver in the sun as it bent before them. He saw the brief horizontal lines across the thighs of two of them, and when the lines raised he saw the puffs of smoke snapping back, and in a while heard the reports coming after. The one would be the French fusil because its sound was slobbering and ragged, but the other was commanding and precise, the way that Ellis's rifle always sounded. They would have his pistol, too, and one of them was riding Morton's horse.

The little mare was moving at a flat run, but the sight of Morton's rangy animal made him cut his reins across her flanks. He was bending low above her neck as a reflex to the smears of powder smoke, and to reduce the drag the wind made on him. When the reports had faded off, her trim hoofs beating on the sod became the only sound, and the Indians for a moment had the look of ghosts coming silently.

Then he heard the onrush of the first one, and the sound held more reality than the sight of him, until their paths converged and Davis saw the sun glazing on the copper skin and the muscles moving underneath. The light marked the curving of the drawn bow and the arrow notched, and he ducked low and watched the brave's eyes squint and open as he let it go.

He waited for the flutter of the shaft above his head

before he looked again and saw the brave throw his arm back to pull another arrow from his quiver. At the same time, Davis swung the mare hard and pulled the Patterson pistol from his belt. He drove the mare ahead with sharp kicks and worked the bit again when she was nearly on the other horse. As her head moved over he saw the Sioux broad and big, and he leaned out and fired point blank at the smooth flesh below the quill and beadwork hung around his neck. Then he kicked again, and looking back, he saw the Indian relaxing and spilling over.

The mare coupled into shorter strides as the coming slope rose beneath her. Everything was going past in blurs and flashes and Davis fired at the next brave before he thought of it. He saw him suddenly to the right, like he'd simply taken root and grown. In his surprise he risked a snap shot and saw the Indian jerking as the ball rustled close to him. Then he fired deliberately and the brave dropped the old fusil and lost control of his frightened horse as he grasped the rip appearing in his thigh. When the animal slewed the rider in a twist of limbs, Davis heard the sound of Ellis's pistol in back of him a ways, and then the ball passing near.

There was only the broad sky ahead until the summit of the rise swelled under him and he could see the slope running to a swale and lifting up again. The other two were topping out behind him with Morton's thoroughbred far in front, and when he turned again he heard the labored breathing of the mare.

The sound of her distress and the long reaching of the horse in back gave him a shot of apprehension. He tried to think how far the wagon train might be, the thought running through his head, remembering the miles that still lay between him and the bluffs, remembering the landmarks he might recognize, remembering the vistas of the valley yet to come when the bluffs were left behind. And the mare was failing fast.

In a while he knew she'd never make it; he'd suspected it before, but had kept his mind away from it, and now he knew. Another mile, perhaps, and it was a queer kind of irony that Morton's horse was both the beginning and the end of this. Futility and sadness took a grip on him as he heard the wind bellowing in and out of her and felt the lather soak his leggings; and anger, too, at the irony again, and lack of justice in it.

Of a sudden, Ellis's pistol fired close enough for Davis to hear the sound sharp and clear above the hoofs drumming, and he felt the mare miss a stride and then saw the bright blood coloring the froth about her mouth. The look of it was frightening, sudden and brilliant in the sun, and when his hand found the wound channel near the leg he knew her lungs were gone.

She was running like a gut-shot deer and he knew her life was going out of her as he felt her muscles soften and her legs jolt, and heard her breathing in a blood-drenched blast. Then her gait fell apart and she made a dozen jumping staggers before her legs collapsed. Davis freed his feet before her head went down, and he was ready when the rushing grass pitched up as her shoulders fell and her back buckled under him.

He hit with his body doubled, rolled in a bounce, and felt his pistol spring away. His feet came under him but he rolled again and came up this time with his knife drawn, held low along his leg. The Sioux brave came on a dead run, but the skittish thoroughbred shied as Davis lunged, and the brave lost his balance and toppled off on top of him.

The brave's knife filled his hand and they rolled and wrenched at one another in the dry grass bending underneath them. Davis landed on the bottom with his breath become a vacuum in him for a moment, but the imminence of death commanded strength of every tissue in him. Instinct made a writhing frenzy of his body, and he squirmed and bucked until a twist freed his hips, and he could slide out from under and come erect.

At the same time, the Sioux turned on his knee and leaped in low without pause, the knife slanting up and his free hand reaching out. Davis saw his eyes flat in their sockets and the scar on his face and remembered how he'd done the talking at the smoke, and how the face showed nothing beneath the paint.

Their hips smashed when they swung together and

their free hands fenced for the knife wrists. The brave's blade streaked up from the knee as Davis's hand missed, and the point caught his leather shirt above the belt line and laid it open to the shoulder. He caught the flicker of the blade breaking clean past his face as he reached again and that time caught the wrist and bent it back. The brave shoved against him and Davis smelled the unwashed stink of the chest pushing moist against him, and felt the leg coming sly behind his own.

Then the Sioux jerked his leg, and expecting it, Davis raised his own quick, and as the shoulder rammed him hard he relaxed and pulled forward swift and sudden on the arm. He jerked quick as the brave tilted over, and kept jerking until the brave let go his wrist in trying to catch himself. Then he stepped back again and swung the knife down and brought it up and saw the astonishment in the dark face, and the cry trying to come, but frozen there. He pulled the knife out and drove it in again, and when the brave loosened up and turned, he pushed him so he fell over on his back and the knife came out clean.

He stood with the wet knife making stains on his leggings, his breath sobbing through him, staring at the brave. So weak he was, it came to him how old he'd suddenly become, how turned to water he was inside, how luck had won the fight, not any skill he might have had. He had the feeling of some old bastard mewling in his mug of wine and staring into yesterday, and thought of what the years had done to him, the years behind the plow, the five years living quiet on the farm with Belle. The weakness and the gone years and Ellis's death engulfed him in their loneliness as he stood gasping in the lonely land. Even the anger at the cause of this was gone as the loneliness and sadness had their way with him. And, of a sudden, he wanted Belle; he wanted to be back with Belle, given she would have him. Of a sudden, everything resolved itself; he'd learned what he had come to find. He could no longer justify his running off alone, and he wondered if it took this chase and fight to make it clear and understandable.

Slowly, he came out of it; he saw the pistols on the ground, his and Ellis's, and he pushed them in his belt. When he looked around he saw the fourth brave hadn't showed, and thought now he likely wouldn't with the odds changed as they had. The thoroughbred stood off, looking careful at him, but remembering, perhaps, the feel of the water and the sand, recognizing him. He walked over slow, holding out his hand, and when the soft nose nuzzled it he thought to curse the horse, but was weary beyond the effort. It took his remaining strength to work his saddle off the dead mare, and hoist it on the other one.

When he finished that he mounted up and looked around again. For the first time he remembered the three Sioux he hadn't seen, and now he wondered if they'd headed into camp before he'd showed, or if Ellis had taken care of them. The question gave him to wonder if this thing had ended yet.

Heading out, he saw the empty land rolling wide and silent, keeping to itself. Coming from the south, the great birds began to circle overhead.

SIXTEEN

They sat in the dark of the wagon, a dark made deep by the order against the campfires, made close by the feeling which existed now against them as a couple, and between them as individuals. Molly could see her husband sitting near the tailgate looking solid black against the looser blackness of the oval shape behind him, and the attitude of his outline reflected the bitterness of his voice.

"I suppose you hate me, too," he was saying now. "Everyone else does; you might as well make it unanimous."

"No, Thaddeus. I don't hate you."

"Oh, come now. You must. It's the universal occupation now."

"I'm sorry if it disappoints you, but I don't."

"Well, how do you feel?"

"I don't feel anything for you," Molly said, and it surprised her to be able to put her thoughts so clearly and so definitely. It really seemed as though someone else had spoken. "Not any more, I don't."

"What?" Thaddeus said, and she knew she had surprised him, too. Thaddeus was not accustomed to any such frankness from her, and he was not accustomed to a negative reaction from anyone. "You must feel something."

"No, Thaddeus, I don't," Molly said, and now it came to her that even had she designed to make little of him she could not have chosen better. "I neither hate you, nor love you. If anything, I pity you."

"Pity! My God!"

Of course, she had astonished him, as she had known she would, but it was the way she felt, and it was a time for truths, however cruel or unpalatable they might seem.

"Yes. I know it's inconceivable to you that one of your—possessions—should look at you that way."

"Possessions?" She could not make out his face, but she felt him staring at her in the dark.

"Isn't that the way you've always looked at me? A rather pretty, but naïve schoolgirl, fortunate beyond her worth to attract your eye. An ornament to set you off?"

"Rot! My God, rot!"

"It's not either, Thaddeus. I'm no more than one of those horses, as far as you're concerned; I never have been. I'm not your wife, certainly. You don't even want a child."

"Oh, come now, really. Don't tell me you wanted to cross the country . . ." Thaddeus paused with the indelicacy on his lips, and Molly prodded him. She could think very forthrightly about him now, and perhaps the trail had done that to her, too. She knew she had toughened up.

"Go on," she said. "Say it."

"Pregnant," Thaddeus said. "With your body swollen out of shape. You wouldn't want that, would you?"

"Probably not. But that's not the point."

"I was only thinking of you. You might not believe it, but I was. We can have a child if you want one; as a matter of fact, I thought about it just the other day, and before that, too. There's no reason why we can't."

"Yes, there is," Molly said. She was very sure of herself, and it was strange indeed to feel that way. It was strange, too, that it should be Thaddeus groping his way along uncertainly. Perhaps at another time, any time until now, she might have enjoyed this novel status, but she wasn't thinking in terms of triumph or defeat for either of them. It was simply a position she was stating and nothing more.

"What reason?" She felt his eyes trying to read her face, her thoughts, and she wondered if she had heard a hint of ugliness in his tone, as though his mind had gone beyond what she had said, and reached its own conclusions.

"I don't love you; I told you that."

"Did you ever?" There was honest curiosity in him now, and Molly knew he was seeing her as a person, like himself.

"Perhaps not, but I knew I intended learning to when we were married. And I respected you immensely."

"And that's all gone, is that it?"

"I'm afraid so."

She could see his silhouette as he placed his hands on his knees and turned his face toward the darkness beyond the wagon as though he was reviewing all the things she'd said.

"It's Davis, I can tell," he said, and the ugliness was prominent and unmistakable. It was clear to her that he had found familiar ground once more, where he could bully and accuse.

"It's not, either. He has nothing to do with it."

"No? Can you deny you've—seen—him?" He said it slowly, the pace and tone implying the double meaning.

"I don't deny anything, I've seen him, as you say." She was sitting very straight. She had expected this and was determined to see it through; they had better get it all worked out right now. "Twice. Neither one by design."

"A lusty, primitive fellow, I presume."

"I wouldn't be able to say how lusty or primitive, as you say."

"Oh, then it's a matter of degree, is it?"

"Don't put words in my mouth, Thaddeus."

"You deny you love him?"

"Emphatically. He has nothing to do with what's between you and me."

"He has a certain charm, though, hasn't he?" Thaddeus was being sly now, but she ignored it.

"Sometimes. But I don't intend to explore it any further." She had thought about this, too, and saying it seemed to solidify her convictions. Nothing good would ever come of seeing Aaron any more; in a way, she was afraid of him, but she was afraid of herself much more.

"I ought to kill him." Thaddeus said it with intensity, and it occurred to her that he was being very like himself again, taking the matter personally when it really had nothing to do with him at all.

"I wouldn't try it," Molly said, and she went on from that, although she knew she was being cruel, and half-regretted saying it. "He saved your life tonight; for the second time, if you count your buffalo hunt. But certainly tonight. The others would have killed you, if he hadn't stepped in."

Thaddeus was quiet for a great while that time and Molly knew she'd struck a telling blow. She truly regretted the point she'd made because she had no wish to hurt him, and she felt she'd been small in saying it. Then she saw his head slump and his hands lift in the dark to meet his face.

"Oh, Christ. I didn't mean it. Christ, I didn't mean it. How was I to know those Indians might be waiting?"

"The others thought of danger. But you wouldn't listen."

"I never doubted that Ellis could handle it."

"You hated Ellis; ever since we left the Blue, you have. You didn't think at all, except about your horse."

"Well, they got him lost, didn't they?" Thaddeus flared up suddenly, and then subsided. "Christ," he said. Then she felt him staring at her again. "What do you want to do?"

"To do?" She was not sure what he meant.

"Yes. Do you want to leave me, or what?"

"I don't know. I hadn't thought." She was surprised that he should come around to this, but relieved, too. "I simply wanted to get it straight for now."

"It's straight, all right." She saw Thaddeus fill the oval as he rose and put his leg across the tailgate.

"Where are you going?"

"I don't know. For a walk. I need the air. Why do you ask? You don't care."

"Just be careful," Molly said, and she did not know exactly what she meant by that.

After he was gone Molly sat for a long while trying to think of nothing, and then she was trembling all over like a leaf in the wind. She knew it was the reaction from facing up to Thaddeus; she had never done that before on any point, and this time she had done it thoroughly and irrevocably, and it had taken something out of her.

It did no good to try and keep away from it because it kept crowding in, just the way it happened, all of it. Her eyes were staring through the oval where Thaddeus had gone, and it was clear dark; yet the sun was shining redly where she again saw Aaron Davis coming in on the exhausted thoroughbred, his clothes in blood and tatters. And she could see the people coming out and standing as they watched and began to understand; and hear the swell of outrage when they learned of Ellis and the Sioux. One time before, in Cincinnati, she had seen a mob explode in violence, and she had been acutely conscious of the presence of those elemental forces this evening, and except that Aaron calmed them, they might have broken out.

She was sitting still, but when the climactic moment appeared in her memory again she rose and made her way to the tailgate, reaching over with her leg, and letting down. She needed air, herself, tonight, she needed room, she needed space. The wagon was a stifling place to be, confining and depressing, both.

She felt the wideness of the dark, and the depth of it, walking slowly beside the wagon. She felt it going on and on, and the room it gave her. It was jet black all around except where the rising moon cast the first of its illumination upward in the east, far along the river. There were no fires, and it was quiet, too, for it was late. It was strange to be walking through the camp where no sound came, save the movements of the stock, and no glowing embers to mark the places where people cooked, or ate, or sang. There had been no cooking after dark, and there had been no singing either. Everyone had turned in early with their sadness for the pilot, their sullenness for Thaddeus, and their apprehension for the Sioux.

She came around the wagon, climbed the tongue and chains, and stood on the outside of the circle, looking south. She could not yet see the bluffs, but she could feel the evil emanating from them; they were full of horror for her now. A word here and there had given her the tale of Aaron's chase and battle; the graphic etching of Jim Ellis lying mutilated beneath the bold and glaring sky, and the great birds bending down to feed.

Then she stood transfixed as she became aware of the movement in the grass and saw the figure rising dim and huge beside her. She felt her whole body fill with the scream coming up, but the scream choked out as the arms encompassed her, as the hand cupped against her month, as the weight bore her down. She thought of bronzed bodies and their nakedness, their filth defiling her; she thought of Ellis in the grass, she thought of hot, groping hands, of knives and axes, she thought of violation, and she felt the scream glowing through her silently again, like heat lightning far off in a summer storm.

"Hey! Calm down! My God, calm down. Hey!" She heard the pleading whisper, but the words didn't register, and still she struggled.

"Hey! It's me, Emmet. Take it easy. You were smack against the moon, an' there's Sioux out there!"

That time she got the meaning of the words still coming in the harsh whisper, and felt her head being turned, and then saw the definite brightness of the moon rising in the east.

"Oh." It was a sob coming out of her as she understood, as the hand freed her mouth and the arms came away, and she relaxed by stages. "Oh. I didn't know."

"I didn't mean to scare you, but I had to pull you down without noise; they're right out there. Did I hurt you?"

"No, but you scared me half to death." She was coming around again, aware of the buoyant Emmet close beside her, and anger beat where the fear was ebbing out. "And you were rough enough."

"I'm sure sorry, but there was nothin' else to do." Emmet was talking in his whispers, still, and pulling on her arm to get her back beneath the wagon where the moonlight wouldn't fall. "You shouldn't have been out here in the first place."

"Isn't it my business where I choose to walk?"

"Sure is, if you can get along with an arrow through your gizzard."

Molly was trying to right her clothes, to smooth her hair and get arranged, but the arrow stopped her cold. All the waspishness went out of her, as though he'd spoken of the Sioux for the first time just then.

"Here? Out here?" It was incredible; there hadn't been a sound all night. She tried to find his face, looking for a smile, a joke. From what she knew of Emmet, it would be like him to fool about this.

"Uh huh. Right out here." He was smiling, all right, but it was no joke. "Half a dozen, anyway, maybe more. I thought everybody knew."

"We were in the wagon," Molly said. "We knew about the fires, but there weren't any Indians here, then. Are they going to make trouble?" She was alert again, the wild surge of terror, and the following anger, gone.

"Don't look like it. Only scouts out there now. We got 'em well-marked; a heap of guards on the job."

"Praise God for that," Molly said. "But they're planning something, aren't they?" In her mind's eye she saw the pilot twisted in the grass again, the ground torn and dark with blood.

"Mmmm—hard to say right now."

"They won't attack us in the morning?"

"Ain't likely. They're just lookin' us over now. If they was Dog Soldiers they might."

"Dog Soldiers?" Molly wondered if Emmet was

playing with her.

"Cheyenne war society. They're always ready, an' they camp together. Takes Sioux longer to get set up. Even on the buffalo grounds they're scattered out."

Molly thought before she spoke again. "I suppose Aaron knows all that."

Emmet laughed softly in the dark as though he'd recognized a reticence or hesitation in what she said. "He knows, sure. If they come at all, it'll take a day or two; the bunch that was here before, that got Ellis, was young an' the war societies got the say about anything big."

"But they're out there now." It was a fact, inescapable.

"They're lookin' us over, all right, but they still got to make their minds up. The Sioux make a heap of talk afore they do anything."

Molly wasn't following him too closely now; the talk of the pilot had made her mind move off. "I'm sorry about Jim Ellis. I liked him so much."

"He was a nice man, that's certain." Emmet spoke it quietly, the understatement making the feeling in it bigger.

"I feel responsible somehow. It might have worked out different if I hadn't told Thaddeus I'd dirtied the horses."

"No, it wouldn't; it'd only happened sooner."

"I hope you're right; how awful." Molly felt a wave of sadness moving over her as she thought of everything. It was all piling up on her, on everyone. "What will happen now? About a pilot, I mean? Will Aaron take it?"

"Have to find a new one at Fort Laramie. Aaron says he's never been past the Snake plain, an' anyway, he's turnin' back."

"Back?" It was only a word at first, until she thought.

"At Laramie."

"I couldn't blame him," Molly said, and then she wondered what she felt, relief or more unhappiness. "Thaddeus couldn't have wrecked things better with a howitzer."

"It ain't that so much," Emmet said, and now she was aware of the careful way in which he spoke. "I guess that scrap up there settled his mind for him; he's goin' back to his wife."

"He left her, didn't he?" She did not say desert; all at once she felt more kindly toward the intense hunter who disturbed her so.

"I guess so. Too bad she wouldn't come along. Aaron, he's got a taste for Oregon."

"We women, we never do it right." She was thinking with despair of her own marriage, the blunder she had made by entering into it, the guilt she felt for taking Thaddeus without loving him. And all at once the sadness of herself, and Ellis in the grass, and Aaron going back, and Esther Sisson who had no child to call her own, and even Isaac Piper dead, arose again and swallowed her, and she was weeping.

She felt humiliation for the tears running on her checks, and then she felt Emmet's arm around her shoulders and she didn't care any more for anything. She let her head move over and heard him talking through her misery.

"Come on, now," she heard him saying, "ain't no time for that. Lemme tell you a yarn I heard," and when she said nothing, but only wept in silence, he said, "A train was one time comin' over the dry stretch 'tween the Little Blue an' the Platte. Dark was comin' on an' the captain had his eye out for a beddin' ground, when all at once there showed an old Pawnee, who was lookin' for a feed. Seein' a chance to build some character, an' bein' well-meanin' anyway, he done his best to please. Sure, there was a place just ahead, he put it to the captain. Plenty good grass for the whoa-haws—an' then he kind of scratched his head—but no water where the goddamns could camp."

"Oh, dear," Molly said, and the tears had stopped and she was dabbing at her eyes. "Thank you, Emmet. Thanks ever so much."

"That's all right. I got a lot more."

"I've heard that." She was smiling now as she looked at him. She was grateful, and she felt pleasant being here with him. Maybe it was because they were of an age, or because they were each alone, though in a different way; but it was good, a natural kind of thing, and she didn't feel self-conscious or uneasy.

"I'll tell you more sometime," Emmet said, and now they were sliding beneath the wagon toward the inside of the circle. When they stood she thanked him again and felt the warmth going to him with her smile.

"It's all right. Feller likes to have an audience." Then he took a look around before he headed off. "How you fixed for buffalo chips?"

"Buffalo chips?" Molly said, and then it came to her. "You!"

"Uh huh." He was smiling hard. "Some gals like flowers, but they won't cook a meal."

"Oh, dear," and she felt the laughter coming. "I didn't know. I knew it wasn't Thaddeus, and it wasn't at all like Aaron."

"Me, all right. Stories an' chips. That's me. I'll sneak some more to you, first chance I get."

"You don't have to sneak them any more."

"No?" and she knew he wondered, and in a way so did she. It was ridiculous and absurd, the chips and the way she felt all at once.

"No. If you want to, just bring them any time."

Emmet flipped his hand as he walked away, and Molly watched him. She was trying to think how long it was since happiness and laughter had been a part of her. She wondered if it was wrong, in the midst of grief and trouble, to feel young and foolish once again.

SEVENTEEN

Andy held the wagons in the circle until full light before he let them move. It was the same with the stock going out for the morning graze; nothing left the camp before every detail of the country roundabout was clear to see. For his own self, he'd rather sit and let them come, if that's what they were going to do; it wasn't bad here, there was grass enough, and the wells would go awhile before the water turned. Another train might come along behind them any time, and that could swing the tide should the Sioux decide to strike in force.

On the other hand, Fort Laramie wasn't getting any closer stickin' here. Suppose the Indians should have it figured out, holding off until the wells were sour and everybody sick? And the chance that another train would not show up was just as good as the other way around. Nor were the Sioux likely to jump them in the pass, so Davis said; they liked room to move their ponies in. Maybe on the other side they would, but Laramie would then be closer by another day. A risk, sure, but as big a risk to stay and sweat it out. Hell, a man risked something every time he took a breath.

"Best to keep movin'," he said aloud, and Esther turned her head to smile at him. The wagons were reaching toward the high rocks and the river was far away.

"Are you still fighting with yourself, Andy?" And, of course she knew he was; he could tell by the smile, and the way she said it, gently critical. "It's the right thing to do; everyone agrees."

"I know they do; I only hope we ain't figured wrong, is all. It adds up right, what we're doin', but you can't count on nothin'."

"Then set your mind at rest about it. You decided on the facts you had. Nobody could have done it different. If something happens it's not your fault."

"I know; I just wouldn't want to be the cause of anyone gettin' hurt, or worse." Somehow that had stood out in his mind more than ever in the past twelve hours, the chance of doing something wrong and getting people hurt or killed on account of it. "Seems to me we've had enough of that."

Esther was walking with him, aside of Star, and she didn't comment, but he knew she was thinking of Jim Ellis, too. He was in the minds of everyone, the pilot was, and his way of death, chasing a goddamned horse. It would make him go cold and brittle all over, the thought of that; and because the feeling was unnatural for the way of him he'd find himself scarce believing anything like that had really happened. He'd be half-expecting Ellis to show again along the line, until the sight of Davis coming in would fill his mind again. That, by God, was real enough.

He thought of Davis now, and looked for him. It was

too bad Davis was turning back at Laramie, but he couldn't very well object to it. The way that Davis had put it up to him made a part of him rather pleased with it, even though he knew it meant trying to find another hunter, too. He supposed he had a sentimental streak in him which made him glad a man should stick it with his woman, no matter what; and Lord knows Esther had taken satisfaction in it. Funny how a woman set such store on the way that other women and their men got on.

With Esther in his head, he glanced around and saw her riding in the wagon now, the Piper boy beside her. The way was rougher as the trail pitched into the bluffs and rocks and it was good she saved her strength instead of squandering it afoot. The look of her, though, told him she was thinking of the boy, too, the fondness she'd felt growing for him, and the emptiness she'd feel when Nellie took him back at Laramie, and was spending all the time she could with him.

Andy knew he'd thought about it, too, but felt himself more favored with logic than a woman was. Young Jamie had a glow of health about him now, was eating good and getting stouter on account of it, and seemed more responsive every day. More than once Andy'd caught himself imagining how it could be when the boy was older, hunting with him, fishing, maybe, or working on the farm they'd have in Oregon. But he'd always come around again and call himself a fool for having thoughts like that. Sometimes, by God, he could be as bad as Esther.

He walked awhile yet, but as the palisades bulked higher, he got to feeling fidgety with the closeness of them, and he went around behind the wagon and got his saddle horse to ride the line. Far away, he saw the last of the wagons rising into the pass.

He rode to the east first and saw the empty valley, relaxing in its vastness, its eternity of age, and the men of the rear guard coming on, but still distant and spread wide. He could see their rifles resting at the ready across their saddlebows, and the alertness in the way they sat with their heads cocked like they were looking up, taking care against surprise.

It was a reassuring thing to see, Andy thought as he headed west again, past the wagons heaving through the pass. It almost seemed the people were sharper than before, as though the reality of Ellis's being gone for good was making them rely more on what they'd learned these months themselves. Trouble sure was nothing to go looking for, least of all the kind that Indians could make; but on the other hand—and he hoped it wasn't wrong to think so—trouble was the best thing to get a bunch of folks to pull together.

When he came back up among the leaders he got a glimpse of Davis riding far ahead, and when the hunter turned his head, Andy waved and made his horse move faster.

"How we doin', Aaron? Look safe, does it?" Andy slowed again when he came beside the other man. He was aware of trying to make light of what he said, but he knew he wasn't fooling anyone.

"Safe as can be, Andy; we're doin' fine. I got men to hell an' gone up the line."

"There's a crowd in back, too. Can't do no better, I guess."

"Not for now. We'll get through, all right. I don't look for anything."

"Until later, I suppose," Andy said, and he gave a short laugh, knowing he was coming sidewise to the matter and feeling self-conscious on account of it.

"Could be, later on," Davis said, "but like we talked it over last night, might nothing come of it at all."

"Now you're tryin' to make me feel good. Did you get it all worked out how many Sioux there were around last night?"

"Come to nine, near as we could tell. There was more'n I thought at first; good thing we held the stock in close."

"And bein' more than what showed up at the smoke it ain't the young bucks' game any more, is it?"

"Can't say about that yet; maybe, maybe not. Next day or so might tell."

The next day or so, Andy thought, and looked ahead, and then up, high up at the cliffs closing in, the intense blue sky far above.

When he looked again he saw Davis smiling at him. "Take it easy, Andy; we got to handle her as she comes."

"I know," Andy said, and felt impatience with himself for the way the doubts and unknown dangers plagued him. But the bluffs wouldn't say, and Davis didn't know, and Andy knew he didn't, either, so to hell with it; he let it go.

After a while he left the hunter and rode on back. He wasn't all the way at ease in his mind about it, but he felt he had certain things straightened out. He thought he could take it now, like Ellis used to, like Davis was doing now. A man couldn't do more than get himself set up as best he could, and then hang on, come what may.

He looked up when he heard the boy call out, and saw the eagerness in his face. "Can I ride in back of you awhile?" Jamie Piper asked again.

"Sure can," Andy said, and he felt something move inside him, pull at him. He brought the horse in close to the wagon and helped the boy swing over. He felt the heft of him again and remembered the day he'd carried him to the wagon in the rain.

"Everything all right, Andy?" Esther asked, and Andy felt her smile embracing them, and knew she was clinging to every bit of this, however temporary it might be.

"Everything's fine," Andy said. "Hang on, now," he

said across his shoulder to the boy.

"Aaron changed his mind about turning back?" She was still smiling, and, of course, she would have to know about that, too.

"I don't guess so; I didn't ask. You sure got that on your mind, ain't you?"

"I know we need him, but I think it's right he goes."

"I guess it is," Andy said, and the horse began to move away. He felt the boy's young body make its light pressure against his own, and the slender arms around his middle, but only reaching part way.

"How you doin', son?" he asked as they headed toward the rear.

"Fine, Pop; I'm doin' fine." It was the first time the boy had called him that, and Andy was astonished at the way it hit him. He felt the thing inside him move again, and this time tear away.

Then he thought again and knew he could never be like Ellis, or Davis either, or anyone who might be like them. He was scared to death, and the boy's arms around him and Esther's smile of wishing they could be that way forever were a part of it. He was just a damned dirt farmer worried sick about these people doing what he said and hoping he was right. If the Sioux came he mightn't have the skill or capability of Ellis or the hunters, but, by God, they would get a fight. Andy felt the fierceness rising up as he thought about it, as he felt the boy hanging on, and saw Esther in his mind again.

They might get through to them, to the boy and Esther, but they'd have to spread his bones and blood over the whole Platte valley first.

EIGHTEEN

The first warning Andy had of it was the far-off shot, long and rolling in the early sunlight of the new day. Then he saw the running horse and Emmet lying flat along its neck as it ran across the valley, clear-marked against the bluffs and hills bending back from the river once more with the pass behind. When his eyes caught the blurred, continuous motion spilling outward from the rocks and hills beyond the hunter, he saw the brief, uncertain images of feathered bonnets and horses plunging in the pall of dust exploding as the horizon came alive when they hit the valley floor; and he knew the Sioux had come.

Andy felt all paralyzed and witless at the imminence of this. It seemed to him that it was only something he had thought about and dreaded, until reality was provided by the first shots dull and distant, and Davis thundering past him down the line. Then it came to him that he was moving, too, that he was riding in a broad turn with his arm raised so the wagon men could guide on him.

He forgot to be afraid for anything, no matter what,

in the confusion and the noise as he got the wagons turning. There was a second when Esther and the boy raced across his mind, but they were gone again when he saw the Sioux clear and heading down, fanning out around the wagons. He heard the shooting plain and near, and then the wild, wild yelling, that like to made his spine twist for the sound of its not being like anything natural or human.

As he made the turn wider he saw the Indians swinging toward the livestock trailing on behind, and he knew the wagons would have a breather while the Sioux were busy with the animals. Already, the frightened cattle had begun to mill, and when the braves got in among them he saw the dust kick higher, and a long, pale flash coming through it as a drover fired. Then he saw an Indian throw his arms out wide and start to fall as the ball took him in the body, and then the cattle broke and ran and the Indian tumbled into the midst of them as the horse was caught and carried with the tide. Andy felt himself go half-sick inside at the sight of the Sioux firing into the cattle running wild, and if he was glad for anything just then, he was glad he had the Star ox in the yoke.

Everything was going fast and there was firing from the wagons now. The circle was about completed, and the lead team stopped already. Andy waited with his pistol drawn while the oxen were removed and the chains and tongues were fastened to the wagon up ahead. Then he rode on back around the circle, staying on the outside; the fighting was still around the animals and he had time to see that things were going proper with the wagons.

It seemed like he had the capacity to notice things and think about them and still keep moving and doing what he should. Once he saw Davis in the middle of it, far off where the herd had scattered, and when he turned again he caught a swift glance of Esther and Jamie on the ground, piling boxes up behind the wagon. He could hear his own voice shouting as he rode on and took these things in. He could hear himself yelling to the men to hurry up, to get the oxen off and in the circle, to get the tongues hooked up, to get the kids and women under cover.

He became aware of the increase in the shooting all around him. He saw the powder smoke coming from beneath the wagon beds, and the ragged flame around the muzzles of the guns, and now the arrows going over.

It came to him the fight was spreading out, and all at once a brave came close to him and swung his war club back. Andy slewed around when he heard the horse running hard and saw the brave's month open in a yell and the paint streaks on his body and his face. At the same time, the muscles in the brave's chest corded as his arm came around and Andy saw the sunlight slanting on the blade in the clubhead as he ducked beneath the arc of it and fired into the painted chest. When his horse turned again he saw the war bonnet streaming on the ground as the brave went over, and he marveled at the lack of feeling in him for having killed a man.

Suddenly the air felt alive with the sing of rifle balls, and the sighing sound of arrows flying in. He felt a shaft ricochet off the cantle of his saddle, and he realized the Indians had got around to this side in force and were coming for him. They became a wave of feathers shaking and the sound of whooping, and apprehension took a grip on him for the first time as he rode, looking wildly for an opening. Then he came around farther and cut in sharp when he saw Emmet standing on a grounded wagon tongue with his arm raised and his mouth shaped in a shout that was lost upon the horses coming in. Andy kicked his horse straight ahead and saw the blur of the canvas tops to either side, and the tongue coming up as the men raised it as he passed. When he swerved around he saw another brave trying to ride him down through the opening, and above the noise heard the clear sound of impact as the horse smashed full against the tongue. Then he looked again and saw the brave pinwheeling to the ground, and Emmet shooting him before he could recover.

Andy turned his horse in with the oxen and such other stock as the Indians hadn't run off. He felt weak and breathy, of a sudden, as he lent a hand to the building of the barricades, as though he'd run a long ways afoot and wasn't used to it. His legs and arms seemed inadequate and spindly-like when he hefted on the barrels and boxes, and when the need for talk arose his voice had a queer, thin pitch to it. It made him think he must be acting like a kid hardly dry behind the ears.

He settled down slow, and looked around him as he moved the boxes here and there. The surprise was gone, and the wagon people were catching up. A lot of them were lying beneath the wagons, and a good fire was beginning to come from them. A kind of rhythm was being established as the men fired, and the boys and women served the new loads as they were needed.

There was confusion yet, but the shock of it was over. Andy knew they were accepting the idea of the Sioux making a run at them, and that they'd make the best of it. There was still some aimless running here and there, and one of these men went over as Andy hunched on by him, an arrow shaft taking sudden root in his upper leg, and the man stopping like a dead man in his tracks and falling over as another man turned quick and caught him in his arms. An arrow was a frightening thing to see, Andy thought, worse than a bullet hole somehow; and a knife and tomahawk were just as bad. Something about a sharp and ripping edge that made the flesh crawl just to think of it.

He kept low, humping along from barricade to barricade; scooting across the openings between the wagons, talking to the people, seeing were they fixed for ball and powder, seeing were they keeping down as best they could. Telling them to shoot the horses if they couldn't hit the braves; no sense in wasting ammunition, and a Sioux afoot was an easier target than one upon a horse. Maybe he could fort up behind a fallen animal, but there'd come a time he'd have to show himself.

Toward the middle of the day some of the Sioux tried to make a breakthrough. The first Andy knew of it was Davis shouting at him and giving him a come-on with his arm, and as he scrunched against the wagons to make a run for it he saw the first braves coming toward the opening between a pair of wagons. He heard the shrill yells as he began to run low toward Davis and the other men, and then he swerved aside as the first horse leaped high above the tongue and chains, the hide frothing and the eyes in a glaze of fear. He got a quick look at the brave's streaked face and the war axe already swinging.

Then the animal dropped its hind feet in the chains and spilled on over, and now behind, Andy saw the other four or five coming on and piling in, some going over, but falling and smashing, too, with men and horses everywhere, with dust and screams arising, and the smell of powder smoke and the noise of guns exploding.

Andy waded in aside the other men, trying to see

what he was doing, trying to figure out if he felt fear or what. Everything was stepping up in pace again, and was so disorganized he couldn't keep track of what was happening any more. He felt the hard shape of his cap-and-ball in one hand and the bone grip of the sheath knife in the other, but there was nothing definite about his use of them, only the awareness of the pistol jerking when he fired, and the knife moving out in front of him and sometimes jarring as it hit, of his shoulder ramming bone and flesh, and of the yelling all around and the dust that choked him and made it impossible to see.

Then he sensed the wagon men getting the grip of them and felt the Sioux give way as the crush against them grew. He heard Davis give a wild shout aside him, and the tail of his eye saw the hunter's knife come down and rise again. A part of the shout got into Andy and he got the smell of victory and boldness in his nose. The excitement of the Indians falling back took hold of him as he fired continuously into the nakedness in front of him, and struck out blindly with the knife when the gun ran dry. He was thinking now of Ellis and of Oregon and of Esther and Jamie Piper lying behind the wagon, and he was filled with ferocity as he drove the knife and clubbed the pistol in a sweeping arc.

Andy sat on the upturned keg with the can of coffee in his hand and watched the Indians milling and arguing among themselves far off where they'd withdrawn to be out of rifle range. The talk of the other men who'd gathered near moved around and over him, but he was still wound up and more aware of Esther watching him than he was of them.

"I've got more coffee, Andy," she was saying to him, and he could tell she was being careful of him, and that the fighting was responsible.

"This is fine," Andy said. "This is all right. I've got plenty. Ask the others." He knew he was speaking in jerky phrases and he still saw himself bracing against the nakedness, the pistol pounding and the knife blade flickering in the sunlight.

He tried to pull himself together and make it smoother, but still she watched him in her secret way, as though she saw a new side of him revealed to her and she was trying to get accustomed to it. "Are you all right?" he asked her. "How's Jamie?"

"We're all right, Andy. We're doing fine. We're perfectly safe behind the boxes." Esther's checks were smooth and lifting with the smile.

"I guess some have been hurt." Andy looked around, trying to add it up. He saw the people resting where they'd fought, stretched beneath the wagons; and the dead animals lying with the arrows sticking out of them at crazy angles. Some of the younger boys were dressing them, against the time they'd bloat, and he knew he should have thought of that himself, but he was still disorganized, half at rest and the other part in the thick of battle yet.

"There've been a few, but I don't think anyone's been killed. Folks are keeping under cover pretty well."

"That's the best way," Andy said, aware of saying the obvious. He was still looking at the animals, at the oxen and the saddle horses and the few milk cows that had been brought inside the circle before the Indians had hit them. They were all staked out near the wagons so they wouldn't run or kick things up.

"Well, what now?" The voice cut clear across Andy's thoughts and when he looked again he saw Mabry, worried and apprehensive, asking it of anyone who might have the answer.

"It's pretty much up to them," Davis said. "They'll be back again."

"We await their pleasure," Emmet said, and Andy had the idea it was Emmet's pleasure, too.

"We ain't doin' so bad, for folks that ain't much used to it." It was Gideon Drew speaking in his dry, nasal way and smiling underneath his arched nose. "Ain't got no killed yet, which is more than they can say."

"We haven't got but five of them," Emmet said, as though it were scarcely a dent.

"Plenty of wounded, though," Davis said, "and that means something."

"Is that all?" Andy was surprised at the low number of Indian casualties. He was thinking of the melee when the Sioux had broken through. It seemed to him he'd taken care of half the Nation by his own self still, only three had fallen to the lot of them that time. And nearly everything else meant a running shot.

"It ain't many," Davis said, "but I doubt they try another rush. That's when they got hurt the worst. They ain't got but forty, fifty altogether, and not all of them is effectives any more. A good many's wounded, an' others unhorsed."

Andy took that in and was surprised again as he thought about it. It seemed to him there must have been a million swooping down. It must be that a man fighting for his life figured everything by tens, and was deceived by the particular scrap he was involved in.

"Looks like we're doin' all right, then," he said, and felt the tension casing out of him, as though the end of it was not far off. "Funny they didn't bring more. We're about even up, countin' the boys an' women loadin'. An' we got the edge of 'em, havin' something to hide behind."

"It don't seem to me they sold the idea too well at the buffalo camps," Davis said. "They could raise a bigger crowd if they had."

"Still the young ones?" It was a new slant, and Andy turned it over, looking at it.

"Mostly, it looks like. The fire-eaters, the hotheads; must have been a lot of argument afore they come."

"Sounds like Sioux squabble with themselves as bad as whites," Drew said, and laughed silently to himself.

"They brawl aplenty, sometimes," Davis said. "And good for us."

"What about the wells?" It was Mabry again, with a new worry, but a real one. Andy looked around and knew that Mabry had hit upon a big thing. Everyone was being quiet, wondering, and as he watched them it came to him the gathering had grown; even Thaddeus Morton was lingering on the fringe. The look of him was bedraggled and discouraged, and Andy could almost feel sorry for him now.

"They could make trouble, all right," Davis said eventually into the silence. "Should they sour we'd have sickness on our hands."

"And the Sioux would finish it," Mabry said.

"They could," Davis said, "if they waited long enough."

"How long before the wells foul?" Andy asked. It was another thing he should have thought about before, and now he wondered why he hadn't. He'd like to think the reason lay with the stunning violence and suddenness of the fight, but he thought he must be dull and stupid, too. It was easy enough to excuse himself by saying a man couldn't think of everything, but he knew that a man who was captain should.

"I don't know," the hunter said, and he paused before he went on with it as though he thought someone else might supply the answer. "But we can't sit here forever," he added when no one did.

"I been thinkin' maybe another train might come along," Andy said. For the lack of wits, he could supply hope, perhaps.

"Others behind, sure enough, but we can't count on 'em, can we?" Mabry said.

"How about an Army column?" It was Drew this time, looking far off, as though the wish might be father to the substance.

"Can't count on that neither," Mabry said, and Andy wondered if he didn't relish being disaster-minded.

"There's Fort Laramie, then," Andy said.

"Can it come to us?" Emmet was having a good time and nothing was going to spoil it for him.

"They got men there," Andy said, following it up and wondering if he'd fallen onto something. "Ain't soldiers, no, but maybe enough to break this up. An' it's only forty mile."

"Take night to do it," Davis said, but he was interested. "Night's the only time a rider'd make it, 'less he rode a bolt of lightning."

"Something to think on, though," Drew said, and hearing the tall man say it made Andy feel better toward himself.

"And in the meantime we got the best of it," he said. Then he stopped dead in the middle of his next thought as the warning gun sounded dull and booming in the quiet.

"That's for us," Davis said, and the others who were

sitting got up, and started moving off. Between the wagons, Andy saw the Sioux in the distance, mounting up and swinging out again.

The other men were running for the wagons as the Indians began to whoop and fire, but Davis was the last to go, and Andy caught him before he left.

"What about it?" Andy said. It was all right to joke and make brave in the crowd, but now he wanted something definite.

"Hard to say, Andy." Davis held his rifle and looked away at the Indians riding in the sun and dust.

"We can hold out, can't we?"

"Until the wells foul, sure. Beyond that I don't know. I keep thinkin' there's a way out, but I don't yet know what it is. Maybe if it shows itself, I'll know. I wish Ellis was here, goddamn it."

"I do, too," Andy said, "and I don't mean nothin' against you by sayin' it."

"I know that—hell," and Davis laughed. Then he looked around again. "If it comes to it, I'll take that ride to Laramie tonight, given that sonofabitch will lend me a horse." Davis didn't have to designate the sonofabitch he had in mind.

"I wouldn't ask you to," Andy said. "Best to draw lots, if it's the only thing to do."

"Christ, it's the least I can do, ain't it? Might be you won't think too poorly of me for goin' back."

"I don't think nothin' of the sort," Andy said. He felt

indignant that Davis should think he might.

"I know," and Davis was laughing at him now. "I'll go; whatever you think; how's that?"

"I'd rather put it off 'til there ain't no other choice; something might develop meantime." He was thinking again of Ellis going off so easily, and what had happened. He wondered if he could have stopped the pilot by speaking out more strongly than he had.

"That's right," Davis said, looking away again, "something might. But this country ain't noted for its miracles."

NINETEEN

Andy kept that in his head, the wells fouling and the Indians maybe waiting for just that thing to happen, and someone, Davis likely, going off to Laramie to get relief for them. It put a new face on the way things shaped up, and made their relative security against a direct assault a short-term proposition. They could handle nearly anything the Sioux could do in force, but a siege was something else again.

He wondered if the Sioux had worked that out already. It seemed to him they kept their distance more than in the morning. They were riding in a great, wide circle around the wagons—the mounted ones—moving only fast enough to make a shot at them difficult, and reaching down beneath their horses' necks to return the fire. The downed ones were forted up behind the slaughtered animals, only a feather of them showing now and then, or a puff of smoke or an arrow streaking out when they lifted up to shoot. The whole thing had a patient, leisurely look to it, like the Sioux had it figured out they'd be there a good, long while, and didn't mind the wait.

It made him nervous just to look at them, and think beyond. He moved around more, keeping busy, trying to keep his mind from dwelling on trouble. It was in the air, though, like it lived in everybody's mind. He could tell it from the slower pace of fire coming from the wagons, as though the people were in agreement with the Indians on the time involved; like they were saving up for something coming later on.

It came to him the air had more than the feeling in it now. It had the stink of the horses and the oxen emptying themselves within the circle. The dead ones were butchered, and the entrails taken care of, but the live ones had their own way of fouling things. The water level in the wells was high, and would the animal waste seep into them? And what about the bloating death outside the circle? Christ, he wished he knew the answers.

"Christ." He said it aloud that time. He was lying underneath the wagon again with his rifle laid across a roll of bedding, and Esther looked at him quickly when he spoke.

"I doubt He'll lend a hand to that tone of voice." She was smiling, but he knew she meant it.

"I'm sure gettin' awful, ain't I?" Andy said. "I can't even think any more, but what I got to cuss. Must be a sign of something bad."

"Oh, you'll get by. I'm not too worried yet."

"Aren't you, now?" It was good to joke with her like this. She was always calm and easy, and never full of jumpiness, like he had gotten lately. It must be women took things more in stride than men. A man always got himself full of blow and bluster when things got hot, but women—Esther anyway—never seemed to change much one way or the other. Maybe 'cause they got the short end of it a lot, they learned to keep their troubles under cover.

She looked away before she spoke again, and Andy wondered if she was thinking of what the Indians were going to do. The idea was progressive and his contemplation of her face made him very much aware of the pistol in his belt, and the two balls he would save, for her and Jamie.

"Is Aaron going to ride for Laramie?" The tragedy of his thoughts had gathered him into them and she had to speak again.

"Aaron?" Andy said it vaguely, and looked at her.

"To Laramie. You were talking of a rider going."

"Oh." Andy moved the hammer of his rifle. "I don't know. He said he would. I don't want to send him, though. I'd rather go myself." Then he stopped as she began to smile again. "What's so funny?"

"I was thinking of you riding full tilt on a horse to Laramie."

"Oh? You think I couldn't? I bet one of Morton's would get there good enough, at night."

"Not with you on it, Andy. It'd break in half."

She was still smiling, and he wondered if she was making fun of him, or was simply making her opposition felt in a novel way. Then all at once the new sound came to him, and he turned around, and saw the shining chestnut horse with the rider up, backing off to run.

"Thaddeus Morton!" It was Esther said it, in vast amazement.

"What? He's goin' to run the tongue between them wagons!" Andy heard his own voice, and thought that Morton's being out there was incredible, but there he was.

They were standing, suddenly, and Andy became aware of the lull, as though everyone had seen, and knew now what was going to happen. Knowing somehow without being told that the officious man whose ways they could never understand was going to try the run to Laramie in daylight.

Andy shouted and heard the stillness after it as the animal received the heels of the rider in its flanks and began to move—soaring, it seemed to be—across the ground before the wagons, and rising like a bronze light across the tongue and chains with yards to spare. Then hitting on the far side, and stretching out, with the Sioux yells shrilling and voracious; and the shift among them as the Indians started toward him.

When Andy saw Davis running for his horse, and heard him shouting for the rest of them, he knew the hunter had seen an opportunity in this, and he ran for his own and mounted up. Everything had changed again and he was aware of shapes and movements that were only fragmentary in their detail as he joined the others on the dead run heading through the gap where a tongue had been let down. It was almost like his coming in again, everything in blurs and shouts and hoofs pounding and faces that he recognized and then were gone again, except that he wasn't alone this time and they were heading out.

He felt there must be twenty of them by the way they spread, but he couldn't be sure of anything just then. He was trying to remember what he'd heard about an Indian's reaction to surprise, but couldn't clearly, except he knew that Davis was acting on it now because the Sioux were occupied with Morton, unsuspecting. The Indians were still a hundred yards away, but the wagon men were coming on the flank and when the range had shortened, Andy fired with the others and saw the heavy fusillade strike the Indians broadside on, and the horses leap and plunge in panic, and the swirl of disorder as the dead and wounded braves fell into them.

The wagon men slammed into them before they could recover and Andy had the clear thought that this was a. moment for a squad of cavalry, for a three-foot saber, and then he thought of nothing clearly any more because his pistol fired and he was into it. It was all impressions on a base of sound and violence. He saw a hand axe rise and fall, and a length of trace chain whine and whirl, and a brave ride off crazily with his head half off, the severed veins spouting blood and the body tilting on the horse. He felt the pistol hitting into his hand as he fired at anything without a shirt, and his legs bruised and hammered from contact with the turning animals. He saw the gray haze of the powder smoke and smelled the acrid bite of it; he saw the bare backs bent and shining in the sunlight, the buckskin leggings, the quills on the dark chests striped with red and black, the plainsman's hats, the feathers whipping, the sweat and blood-drenched homespun shirts, a bow drawn, the open months, the yellow teeth, the eyes—scared and animal and brutal; he saw blood on the blade of his sheath knife.

And then he saw the Sioux break, saw them break and try to rally, and break again; and with the second breaking there was only flight and rout and those that remained alive and mounted put their horses toward the south, crying weird cries, and falling, some of them, as the firing from those that followed pulled them down.

The men came back from the hills by twos and threes,

in small groups. They came slowly, walking or riding, as they chose, and now and then one might stop to put the end to a wounded brave. Andy saw one of them sawing away at a scalplock with his knife, but he could look at that now without thinking one way or the other on it.

He went afoot toward the circle, the horse coming along behind him, the bridle on his arm, thinking it was good to be dull inside, unfeeling for a change. It must be nature gave a man a break after a length of time, and he could then take anything without his being amazed, or astonished, or afraid or glad or full of sadness or anything. When he reached that point it all evened out and the good was one with the bad, and elation no different than remorse.

"Whatever else, he had guts, goddamn it." It was Davis spoke, and Andy looked and saw the hunter coming up aside him.

"Who's that?" he said; he wasn't making any efforts at remembering.

"Morton. He must have known he didn't have a chance."

"Yeah. I guess he did have guts." It was too early to think of Morton yet. He could see him lying in the shambles of the fallen horses and the Sioux dead, but that was all. It was just a picture now, with nothing going beyond it. One day he'd have a feeling for it, an evaluation of the man he'd known as Thaddeus

Morton. But not just yet.

"Maybe he was tryin' to square things, somehow." Davis was going on with it, but Andy only shrugged because the reason for the impulse and everything about it were still meaningless for him.

He looked ahead again when he heard a final burst of fire from the far side, and at the end of it a few remaining Sioux, who hadn't gotten in the skirmish, headed out and rode south toward the hills. There looked to be a handful afoot, too, making off through the grass, and Andy knew they'd get away because everyone was tired of the fighting now, no matter were they Sioux or white.

Then he came through the gap and saw Esther coming toward him. She straightway put her arms around his neck and kissed him, but didn't smother him; she did it like he was simply coming home for supper.

"Andy, I've got coffee for you." She said it in his ear.

He still felt too distant from himself to favor intimacies, and she was being the way he wanted her to be.

"Thanks," he said. "Thanks. Are you all right?"

"Yes. I'm fine. Everything's all right."

"How's Jamie?" He looked around for the boy, but didn't see him.

"He's all right." Esther took her arms away and looked up and Andy gradually became aware of the strangeness in her, of her lips becoming tremulous and her eyes round and large, as though she was balanced on the brink of great emotion.

"Esther! It's the boy!" For the first time since the fight he came alive.

"No, Andy. No, it isn't." Her arms came around his neck again and she pulled his head down, and he felt the sobs going through her before her voice broke. "It's Nellie."

"Nellie?" He waited; he didn't think of anything except the word.

"A stray arrow, Andy. Just a chance. The merest chance; nothing but a stray, as the Indians went away. But it took her." It was all run together, and she was weeping now.

"Nellie killed." He spoke it out loud and he had the awareness now to understand it. And he prayed to God he was not a monster for the meaning he attached to it.

TWENTY

The three men slouched against the adobe wall in the afternoon sun, reclining on the grass with their pipes going. There was a new train coming through the hills toward the Fort, and the people of their own outfit were coming out to watch down below; but the look of these against the wall said they had the leisure now to pick and choose about a thing, and that they inclined to let the world go by of its own accord for a while. Time enough to meet the new folks when they were circled, when the pipes were done. Indolence was a luxury, and five days hardly got a man accustomed to it.

It was enough to laze and watch, and Davis thought of their own arrival near a week ago. They must have looked like this train coming through the hills. He remembered how he'd felt when he'd seen the bleached stockade and the lodges of the trading Indians pitched all around, the piles of buffalo hides, big as haystacks, and the trees along the Laramie. He'd felt his own sigh a part of the great, universal sigh going out of everyone, and after that he'd felt like whooping, and he had, and so had a lot of others.

"It's a train, all right," Andy said in a while, his way with it leaving a doubt as to whether he was pleased or not. "You figure we can join 'em, Aaron?"

"Sure, you can. They ain't no bigger'n what you are, an' as they likely seen the leftovers from the scrap we had they'll be glad of company."

"I suppose they might be, at that," Andy said.

"Be damned fools otherwise," Emmet said.

"Do you think it's the right thing?" Andy said.

"Only way you're goin' to get a pilot. Not much choice here at the Fort; 'less you'd be happy with Matt Daniels."

"Take a wagon to haul his whisky for him," Emmett

said, "from what I hear."

"A pack horse, anyway," Davis said.

"We better join this bunch, then," Andy said. "If we can fix it with their head men."

"Won't be hard," Davis said, and he was thinking now of Andy getting himself all full of worries and concerns again. "They get squared away, we'll go pay a call."

Andy hitched himself farther up the wall before he spoke again, and began it slow. "I'm sure grateful, Aaron, for your stayin' on this way to see us fixed up for a pilot. Everybody is."

"It's all right." Davis tamped the coal of his pipe with his thumb, and frowned at the smoke curling up. "I'd want to know you was headin' out right."

"It's a long way yet, I guess," Andy said, and his voice filled up with the distance still to come.

"Uh huh," Davis said. "It is; to hell an' gone. I ain't worried much about you, though."

"I wish you was comin' all the way," Andy said. "Be good to have you out there, a part of it, like the rest of us."

"I wish I was, too," Davis said, and he was surprised at the strength of feeling that came over him. "I'm goin' back, though."

"A woman sure got a way with a man, ain't she now?" Emmet said, his way of saying it full of lazy humor.

"I guess there ain't anyone knows that better'n you," Davis said, and when he looked at Emmet he knew the color in his face had as much to do with pleasure as it did embarrassment.

"Is it all right, d'you think?" Emmet said, and by the earnest way of him, Davis saw that Emmet had turned the woman talk on his own self, like he wanted to be assured.

"If you don't take her, another man will," Davis said. "Sure, it's all right. Be a fool if you didn't."

"A slick way to get yourself a team an' wagon, too," Andy said. "To say nothing of a thoroughbred horse." Andy had his hat brim down and it was hard to see whether he was smiling to himself or not.

"And a stallion, to boot," Davis said. "Thaddeus must have been thinkin' of you when he rode off on the mare."

"Goddamn it, all I asked was did you think it was all right," Emmet said, flaring up like a pine-knot blaze.

"Why, we're tellin' you, ain't we?"

"Ain't he the fiery son, though," Andy said. "Ought to burn well come his weddin' night."

"Goddamn it . . ." Emmet started in again, but quit when the other two began to laugh, and then Emmet got himself pulled into it.

They all three laughed in deep belly laughs, at length, and Davis was aware of the warmth it left with him. He felt his face ache with the smiling, and inside him was the pleasure, still; and the shadow of regret, too, as he watched the train and thought of what was coming.

Then he pushed that part of it away and looked hard at the wagons coming on across the river to the ground below, and thought to himself, as those beyond must be thinking, and likely saying, too—Fort Laramie.

Fort Laramie. He formed it with his lips and saw the wet and shiny oxen strain against the yokes. Fort Laramie and the easy time, the pleasant days, the hours of laziness for men, the day-long rest and grazing for sore-footed livestock. The Indians dancing their ceremonials around the fires in the evening, the wagon people turning with the fiddle's music, the whisky barrel handy. Young love whispering in the shadows.

The regret took hold of him again, and this time it wouldn't go. It didn't make any difference that he'd made his mind up, that he'd chosen right, he was filled with it now as the new train made his taking leave of everyone so imminent. It sharpened his awareness of the far land still to come, the monumental ranges, and the rivers flowing clear as glass, the sea breasting on the golden shores.

A man could find things to do out there; Andy would, and so would Emmet. Himself, now, was he going on along with them, he could farm and maybe not mind it in such a place, but there were other things that needed doing, too, in a land so young. A whole new country must be built and a man could have his choice of a thousand different ways of pitching in. There wasn't any limit to it.

Then he looked east again, and saw the Muddy rolling onward in his mind. He felt the thick, damp air and smelled the swamp-rot in the silted backwaters where the cattails stirred and the insects forever buzzed on a summer night.

"You want to go down now, Aaron?" It was Andy breaking through his thoughts. "They're pretty well circled up now."

"All right. Might as well."

The three men rose, and slapped the dried grass from their shirts and leggings, and started down the slope toward the wagons where the folks were getting out to stretch.

Davis hoped the mosquitoes would be gone when he returned to Independence.

Esther took her fork from the Dutch oven, put the lid on, and with a stick nudged it into the glowing coals of the cooking fire, where it would simmer until time for supper. She'd already scrubbed herself and put a clean dress on, and was ready to call on the new arrivals. When she straightened up again she looked for Jamie, wondering if she should take him with her, but when she saw him sitting on the hip-shot Indian pony fifty yards away the look of him struck her as so manly she knew she couldn't subject him to the tedium of woman's gossip. Andy's letting him ride the little pinto horse had been a step away from childhood for him, and though Esther had her reservations on the matter, she was wise enough to know she shouldn't express them by tying him to her apron strings.

Really, it was so much like their own selves coming in, she thought as she neared the wagons. Those last miles had seemed like eternity itself, and these folks looked drawn and weary in the same way their own had looked and felt. Fort Laramie was a strange place of swarthy French and Mexicans, of pelts and hides, and fat squaws and braves sauntering with their blankets to their chins, but it was a blessed sight nevertheless, and it didn't matter, any of it, when you were tired and exhausted.

And when you were relaxed and observing once again, it didn't really matter, either. The Indians, the hunters and the other unkempt-looking men you saw were all a part of the West and everything it meant, and there were more to come the farther on you went. It surprised her now to realize she had it all so clear in thought, and felt it must be a process based in natural law. For having once accepted certain other things, her ties with the past had gained a new perspective, and she could now accept these new events and places without her former feeling of defeat and dread.

When she came around one of the wagons and saw

the young woman letting herself carefully over the tail-gate, Esther moved impulsively to help. She was obviously pregnant, and Esther took her arm in her hand to steady her, and when the young woman stood squarely on the ground Esther became aware of the clear skin of her oval face, the very black wavy hair, and the over-all impression of striking beauty.

"You came at the right time," she said, her way of it showing good humor at her condition. "Without an extra hand, it seems to take an hour to reach the ground. Thank you very much."

"Why, I'm glad I came by," Esther said. "I suppose it is a nuisance now, but you'll feel different when you're holding it in your arms, and fixing for it." They were trail people, both of them, and Esther knew it made no difference that they'd never met before. Pretense and talk that only alluded to a thing were left on the east bank of the Muddy.

"Everybody tells me that; I hope it's true." The young woman's laugh was soft and pleasant, and Esther saw her teeth white and even between her lips. There seemed to be a vague resemblance to Molly Morton in her features, though the coloring was different, and Molly lacked a good five years.

"It is," Esther said. "I know." Esther found her mind straying off as she said it, but she could think of Jody now without the overwhelming crush of sadness. "Your first, is it?"

"Yes, and I'm not used to carrying it yet. It's hard to keep my balance sometimes."

"Oh, I know how that can be," Esther said, and though it was far away in time she could still remember. "It must be awful in the wagon all day long."

"It does rock around a lot and makes my back ache so, but there's no help but to hang on."

"Of course there isn't," and Esther found herself feeling almost motherly toward the strange woman for a moment. Perhaps it was because she'd settled all the old griefs and conflicts within herself, and felt renewed again and fulfilled with Jamie. It made her expansive and generous of herself with everyone.

"But it won't go on forever," Esther added when they had moved to sit on the lid of a hump-backed trunk. "You get to Oregon, your husband'll build you a snug house that won't rock, even in the wind."

"I wonder," the young woman said, and Esther was aware of the subtle change, and wondered if it was something she had said.

"I don't know," she said again. She was looking full at Esther, but her eyes were big and round and Esther had the notion they were going through her and away. "He went on ahead. I'm just riding with these people. I don't know where he is."

"And you came alone? You have a lot of courage." Esther marveled at it, and at the same time felt impatience with the footloose husband for letting his wife come after him alone the way she was.

"He doesn't know about this," the young woman said, as though she understood what was going through Esther's mind. "I didn't tell him; he left before he knew."

"You didn't tell him?" Esther said, and she was now conscious of there being something wrong with this, and wondered if she would have stopped at all if she'd known she'd get involved in it.

"We hadn't been getting on very well. I was two months gone when he left. Maybe I could have held him if I'd told him, but I didn't want it that way." She said it all quickly and quietly, but there was a strain of pride running through it, too.

"You'll find him, all right." Esther was being careful how she said it. She hoped she didn't sound pious or anything like that.

"My French blood, I guess; too much pride. He'd hardly gone when I knew I had to follow him."

When Esther didn't say anything, the young woman gave a short, self-conscious laugh, and glanced around.

"He must have gone through here."

"Of course he did," Esther said. "Everybody goes through here." Esther felt less queer about it now that she understood, and action was in prospect. "There haven't been so many folks going by the Fort this year that someone wouldn't remember him."

Then she caught a sight of Andy coming down the slopes with Emmet and Aaron Davis, and the sudden warmth she felt made her wonder if she unconsciously compared herself with the one beside her. Everything was so secure and orderly for her. "I'll get my husband to ask at the Fort about him."

"You're kind, but I don't want to be a lot of trouble."

"It's no trouble at all. He's the captain of our train, and he'll be glad to help." Esther was careful not to make a thing of it.

"You're very kind," the young woman said again. She was staring into her folded hands which lay in her lap, and Esther looked away again. Andy and the hunters had reached the circle and were coming along the line of wagons, and Esther could see their lips move as they talked.

"What's your husband's name, dear?" Esther asked. She still watched Andy and thc others, but when she got no answer, she turned around again and was fascinated and astonished by the radiance she saw. The girl was standing now, her face all of a glow as Esther looked at her.

"Chéri!" She said it softly, and Esther felt her skin becoming cold and her heart lurch as she heard it. "Chéri!" the young woman said again.

Then the men came past the wagon and turned their heads as Aaron Davis stopped like he was an ox that had been poled.

"Belle!" He nearly shouted it, as the girl moved toward him. "Belle! Good gawdalmighty, Belle!"

Andy sat with his back against the wagon wheel, his eyes upon the tip of Laramie Peak where the sun still shone like something melting red and slow upon a hot fire. He felt his lips smiling about the pipestem as he watched the changing colors on the Peak and thought again of the contentment he was feeling.

"It beats all, don't it, Esther?" Andy turned his head and let his look rest on the woman by the fire. He saw the flush the heat made in her face and the shadows in her features from the flames.

"What's that, Andy?" Esther had her Dutch oven out of the fire now, and she was poking at the contents with her fork, and she didn't look at him.

"How things go." He saw the muscles moving in her arm as she turned the fork, and the shades of meaning in her expression as she studied what she'd cooked, and decided whether it was right or not. He felt his smile grow wider as he thought of what it all meant, her fixing for the boy and him.

"You mean Aaron and his wife?" This time she looked up, and it came to him he'd never seen her look so pretty. Maybe it was the way he felt himself, reading beauty into her, but it did seem like she'd bloomed.

"Well, Aaron, sure; though I was thinkin' of it all, I guess."

"Yes, I guess it does beat all, Andy." Esther's face was pensive and he knew she was thinking far away and back, and seeing the train come onward day on day. A part of it got into his own feelings as he watched the mood come over her, diffusing, for a moment, the pleasure in him.

Andy looked away into the open ground and saw the stock feeding with their muzzles in the grass. Still beyond, Jamie was sitting on the Indian pony, riding here and there slowly, as though to see that everything was set and proper for the night. It reminded him of the other person with such an attitude of watchfulness, and when he looked at Esther she was watching, too, and he knew she was aware of it.

"Goin' to miss Jim Ellis," he said to her. "Miss him plenty now."

"Yes. Yes, I know. I even feel badly about Thaddeus Morton."

"I don't guess he could help bein' what he was."

"Maybe not. Andy"—she was still looking out at Jamie moving slowly back and forth—"how do you feel about Nellie?"

"I wasn't glad about her goin', if that's what you mean. But she wasn't near the ma that you are. I wouldn't wish death on no one, but I'd think twice 'fore I wished her back." He had it settled now, but it had taken time.

"That's a man, all right," and though she smiled

when she said it, the pensiveness replaced it and Andy knew she hadn't got it all worked out yet. Motherhood was a complicated business.

Then Esther shook her fork as though that helped her put her mind on supper once again. "I guess you better call him, Andy. It's about ready. And, Andy, don't forget what he asked."

"All right." Andy chuckled to himself and pushed up from the ground. When he moved to the end of the wagon he could see far out and away, the Fort cresting on the rise, the molten summit of the Peak, and the low pile of dark hills to the west. And if he let his mind go on there was the South Pass, the Green, the Snake, and all the other great rivers he had heard about. There were the forests lifting up and the sloping valleys and the arches of the world where the snow lay forever cold and white.

When he looked at the boy on the pony he was struck by the natural look of him against the wildness and the distance that lay beyond, and the thought came to him that already he belonged to it. Himself and Esther, they would lay the groundwork and live their time, but a part of them would always be remembering the land they'd left. But the boy would grow to know the new country, to be sure of it, and to love it, and already he had the look of belonging to it.

"Jim! Oh, Jim!" Andy cupped his hands around his mouth and called it loud, not womanlike, but man to man. He remembered about the name. “Oh, Jim, supper!”

That time the boy heard and Andy saw his hand go up in a wave at him, and then to the side of his face as though there was a yellow mustache he was twisting. Then his arm went straight up and the boy’s head turned to look in back of him as the hip-shot pinto started forward. Andy heard the small voice piping out across the land and saw the arm still raised as though it was a point to guide on.

“Roll them wagons!” The sound of it was clear and brave in the early evening. “Roll them wagons, people; keep ’em rollin’!”

And the pilot brought his train alumbering in to dinner.

Center Point Publishing
600 Brooks Road • PO Box 1
Thorndike ME 04986-0001 USA

(207) 568-3717

US & Canada:
1 800 929-9108